Divinely Designed

Divinely Designed

RACHAEL RENEE ANDERSON

Bonneville Books
Springville, Utah

FICTION

The views expressed within this work are the sole responsibility of the author and do not necessarily reflect the position of Cedar Fort, Inc., or any other entity.

This is a work of fiction. The characters, names, incidents, places, and dialogue are products of the author's imagination, and are not to be construed as real.

ISBN 13: 978-1-59955-324-5

Published by Bonneville Books, an imprint of Cedar Fort, Inc., 2373 W. 700 S., Springville, UT 84663
Distributed by Cedar Fort, Inc., www.cedarfort.com

LIBRARY OF CONGRESS CATALOGING-IN-PUBLICATION DATA

Anderson, Rachael Renee.
Divinely designed / Rachael Renee Anderson.
    p. cm.
ISBN 978-1-59955-324-5
1.Interior decorators—Fiction. 2. Humorous stories, American. 3. American fiction—21st century. I. Title.

PS3601.N5447D58 2010
813'.6—dc22

                                2009032466

Cover design by Angela D. Olsen
Cover design © 2009 by Lyle Mortimer
Edited and typeset by Katherine Carter
Printed in the United States of America

10 9 8 7 6 5 4 3 2 1

Printed on acid-free paper

For my sweet mother, whose love of reading was so infectious. For my sisters, whose friendship and enthusiasm propelled my writing. For my wonderful friend, Shelley, who shared with me her wisdom, time, and talent. For my incredible husband, Jeffrey, his belief in me, and the picture frame he gifted me so many years ago.

And for my own Kennedy. May she grow up to be the beautiful, confident, talented, and strong young woman she has already shown signs of becoming.

❋ Chapter 1 ❋

STRANDED. OR AT least, that's how most girls would feel if they sat alone in a car on a two-lane highway in the middle of the desert. Kennedy Jackson, however, was not like most girls. She was stubborn, sometimes pig-headed, and thoroughly versed in how to change a stupid tire. And yet, that knowledge offered no reprieve to her frustrated spirits; Arizona's sizzling heat did not make her anxious to leave her car.

"Darn you!" she snapped at the front passenger tire. Why did it have to deflate in the middle of nowhere? To make matters worse, the spare tire and tools she needed were buried beneath all the clothes, boxes, suitcases, and the large teddy bear stuffed in her car.

Hoping that procrastination would bring a decrease in the 115-degree temperature awaiting her outside, Kennedy's thoughts drifted to earlier that morning, back in Albuquerque, when she was loading the last of her stuff into her silver '05 Toyota Corolla. Instead of folding all of her clothes and packing them neatly in boxes, Kennedy had left them on hangers and tossed them in the trunk on top of everything else. The back seat of the Corolla was jammed with two overflowing laundry baskets containing clothes she had washed late the night before. On top of the baskets, her favorite comforter and pillows were crammed into the empty spaces, making her rearview mirror useless. And finally, her aged and sizeable computer was smartly placed on the passenger seat, with her monitor securely buckled in place.

"As much as I loathe the thought of you driving alone, it's probably for the best, considering you would have to tie the computer on your roof to fit someone else in here," her mother had said wryly that morning as she peered into the car, her cropped, curly hair blowing gently in the warm breeze. Kennedy's looks and height came from her mother. They each sported rich brown hair, chocolate eyes, and a perfect oval face with an olive complexion.

"I couldn't kick the computer out of its seat!" Kennedy exclaimed with false sincerity. "I'm afraid that any passenger seeking a ride with me would be offered the top of the car—definitely not the seat of my ancient and unreliable computer."

Shaking her head, Olivia smiled sadly at her daughter. "I can't believe that the summer is already over and you're leaving again. It seems like yesterday that you surprised us with the news that you were going to BYU for college. I thought that was bad! But now you're moving away again to start a career. I despise the idea that this move could be permanent."

"Now, sweetie." Kennedy's father placed his arm around his wife and pulled her close. "You knew this was going to happen one day. We should be grateful for such an intelligent daughter that graduated at the top of her class and has landed a terrific job. She's only going to be one state away. At least she's not moving to Australia or South Africa."

Olivia replied with a glare. "Dear, you're not helping."

"What?" Tom exclaimed as if deeply hurt. "I have too helped! Who do you think carried out all these boxes?"

"My point exactly," said his wife, smiling.

Kennedy laughed at her parents as she tossed her purse into the car and turned to say good-bye. She hugged her mom and then reached up to give her dad a hug as well. He was a good foot taller than she was, and what was left of his dirty blond hair had turned gray over the years. Kennedy was proud of her parents. "I am going to miss you both."

"We are going to miss you too, sweetie," Tom replied. "Now you be careful and make sure to call if anything happens along the way."

Thinking of her parents made Kennedy smile, but only until her thoughts drifted back to the present, and she was forced to deal with her inconvenient situation. Groaning, she stepped out of her car and into the convection oven called Arizona.

She took a deep breath and popped open her trunk. After flinging all her unpacked clothes on the top of her car, pulling out all the luggage and boxes, and carefully situating her bear on top of the pile, she finally cleared the trunk and revealed the compartment carrying the spare tire and tools. Thankfully, there were no other cars in sight to witness her disarray, so she shrugged her shoulders, gave a brief sigh, and got to work.

The car was just beginning to rise when Kennedy heard another vehicle approach and pull off the road in front of her. Glancing up, she glimpsed the tail end of a shiny, black Chevy Silverado. She rolled her eyes, wishing fervently that whoever it was would continue on his way, and wiped the perspiration on her forehead. She worked quickly to finish jacking up the Corolla. Her independent nature wanted the owner of the truck to realize that no help was necessary.

Her hopes were dashed when she heard the truck door slam and a deep, male voice ask, "Setting up camp?"

"Looks that way, doesn't it?" she replied dryly.

He chuckled before asking just what she had expected him to: "Need some help?"

Kennedy glanced up to find a startlingly good-looking man towering over her. She was suddenly all too aware of her less-than-flattering attire that consisted of cut-off sweats and a frumpy T-shirt. He looked to be in his late twenties and was over six feet tall, with dark brown hair and a deeply tanned face. His brilliant blue eyes peered down at her in curiosity as he waited for an answer. Not wanting to be caught staring, Kennedy quickly refocused her attention on the tire.

"No, I can manage. But thanks for the offer," she said simply.

"You know how to change tires?" He sounded surprised.

The comment annoyed Kennedy. Did he think that because she was a girl, she couldn't change a tire? What a chauvinist! Chris would never have assumed anything of the kind. Thoughts of Chris brought back painful memories, which made her even more annoyed at this stranger. She cast him a sidelong glance and said sweetly, "Actually, no. I have no idea how to change a tire. Is that what I'm doing?" She stopped jacking up the car and studied her work curiously. "I could have sworn I was flushing out the radiator fluid."

Her comment brought a chuckle, and Kennedy noticed that the irritating man had dimples. He really was handsome. "Sorry," he said, smiling. "I didn't mean to offend you. It's just that all the girls I've known couldn't change a tire if their life depended on it. I was just trying to say that I'm impressed."

"Well, thanks," she said, some of her unkind thoughts washing away with his explanation, but she still wished that he'd go away. It was far too hot for idle chitchat. Rather than obey her silent wish, he shoved his hands in his pockets and casually observed her, a smile tugging at the corner of his mouth.

Feeling his eyes on her, Kennedy glanced up and mustered a friendly tone. "I promise that I wasn't fibbing when I told you that I know how to change a tire. You really don't need to wait."

"So you said." His eyes twinkled in amusement as he continued to watch her work. Kennedy wondered what coconut tree the guy had fallen from. Couldn't he take a hint? He didn't budge or say anything and returned her stare steadily. She finally looked away and shrugged her shoulders.

"Great, now we'll both get heatstroke," she muttered. She was suddenly annoyed with him again.

Kennedy removed the hubcap and began working to loosen the lug nuts. Unfortunately, whoever put the tire on the car last had fastened the lug nuts so securely that nothing she could do would budge them. To make matters worse, her tire disobediently spun each time she attempted to turn the tire iron. Kennedy threw down the tool and kicked her tire with exasperation. Hearing muffled laughter, she turned and glared at the stranger.

"Now would you like some help?" His tone was unrepentant.

Not seeing any humor in the situation, Kennedy handed over the wrench and swallowed her pride. "Fine. You win."

The man chuckled as he bent to lower the jack so the tire would rest against the asphalt and stop spinning. Then, picking up the wrench, he easily removed the lug nuts. Realizing that she could finish changing the tire on her own, Kennedy held out her hand for the tool. "Thank you for your help. It's good to know that there are still some gentlemen left in this world, but I really can do the rest myself. Feel free to return to your air conditioned truck."

Undaunted, the man relinquished the wrench but stayed to watch Kennedy finish. "Are you, in some way, annoyed with me?" he asked quizzically.

"No."

"Then you need to work on your body language." Kennedy ignored his comment, so he continued out loud, as if musing to himself. "Now why, I wonder, would someone be aggravated when a complete stranger goes out of his way to help her change a tire on such a hot afternoon?"

"What are you, a psychiatrist?"

"Right now I'm wishing I were, because then I might be able to figure you out."

"What can I say? I'm a mystery." She shrugged and finished tightening the lug nuts.

"Seriously, what did I do wrong?" he asked. "I'm feeling a little lost here."

Kennedy sighed as she stood up. "Listen, don't get me wrong. I am grateful you came along because I don't think I could have removed that tire on my own. Believe it or not, I'm not usually so cranky, but I really can't stand it when someone, specifically a male, thinks I can't do something because of my gender."

"Please don't tell me you're a radical feminist," he joked as he reached down to grab the flattened tire before she had a chance.

"No, I'm not that extreme, just a little independent." She followed him to the back of her car and lifted the trunk for him.

"I never would have guessed," he replied sarcastically as he reached up to wipe the perspiration from his forehead. He glanced at the things gathered around him on the ground. "How in the world did you fit all this stuff in your trunk?"

Kennedy smiled. "Honestly, I have no idea." She laughed as she bent to pick up the nearest suitcase and tossed it in the trunk. A bag soon followed. When she reached for the teddy bear, he held up a hand.

"Please tell me there's some method to your madness."

"Of course there is. Once everything is in, I jump really hard on top of the trunk to get it closed."

He looked her up and down skeptically, obviously doubting her flyweight frame could do anything of the kind. "I've got a better idea," he said. "How about you hand all your things to me, and I'll pack it for you?"

"I think I've put you out too much as it is. Seriously, I can finish up here."

"You obviously don't know the definition of the word *gentleman* if you think I'm going to leave you like this."

"Okay, okay, you win again." She handed him a box and bent to retrieve a duffle bag.

Taking out the few things she'd already thrown inside, he meticulously began repacking her trunk. "So, where are you headed?"

Not wanting to start a personal conversation with this guy, she said only, "Tempe."

"Really?" He sounded genuinely interested. "What for?"

"If you couldn't guess by looking in and around my car, I'm moving there."

"Why?"

Kennedy handed him another bag. "Are you always such a snoop?"

Shrugging, he grinned. "I like to call it curious."

"Same thing," she responded. "You're just euphemizing the word."

"Well, aren't you an optimist?" he rebutted dryly, rephrasing his earlier question. "So, what brings you to Arizona?"

"A job," she replied, picking up another box and handing it to him.

"What kind of a job?" He fit the box snugly between two bags.

"What is this, twenty questions?" Kennedy said distractedly. She handed over one last bag, watching in wonder as he fit it easily beside a box, threw the remaining clothes on top, and effortlessly slammed the trunk closed. "How did you do that?" she asked in disbelief.

"What can I say? I'm a miracle worker." He leaned back against the car casually, folded his arms, and considered her expectantly. "So are you going to tell me what kind of a job would make you move to Tempe in the middle of the summer? I have to admit, you've intrigued me, and I'm not easily intrigued."

"Okay, fine," she replied, wanting nothing more than to return to her car and crank up the air conditioning. "I just graduated in interior design from a school in Utah called Brigham Young University, and I landed a job as a design assistant for an exceptional, high-profile firm. I'm not usually so lucky. Believe me. I am going to be living with three other girls in an apartment. Even though I didn't get around to running background checks, I'm told they are sweet girls, so you don't need to worry. I'm originally from a suburb near Albuquerque. I have no pets, unless you count Pineapple," she gestured toward the teddy bear, "and I received a speeding ticket last year about this time." Kennedy paused to take a breath. "There, now you know my whole life story—any more questions?"

He didn't attempt to disguise his smile. "If it weren't ridiculously hot out here, I'd keep badgering you for the fun of it, but I'll refrain and let you go."

"How thoughtful," she replied wryly, feeling slightly guilty for her behavior.

Before she could offer any words of apology, he began, "Listen, Miss . . . ?"

"Kennedy," she said simply. "And you are?"

"Braxton Taylor." He smiled, extending his hand. "And I do apologize for plaguing you with my presence."

Allowing a slight smile to touch her lips, she shook his hand and replied contritely. "Believe it or not, I am sorry for being such a grouch. I blame the heat."

"Ah, so what you're saying is—"

"Oh, please don't start analyzing me again." Reaching in her pocket, she pulled out her car keys. "I really do appreciate your help, though. It would have taken much longer if you hadn't come along, so thanks."

"My pleasure." He started walking back toward his truck. Thinking he was finally leaving, Braxton once again surprised her when he stopped next to her car and pulled open the door, waiting patiently for her to get in.

"Wow, you really are a gentleman." Kennedy smiled as she sank into the driver's seat. "Thanks again."

"You're welcome, Miss Kennedy. And I must say that you have one heck of a smile." He winked at the wide-eyed look on her face.

"Here's hoping that we bump into each other once the weather cools down a little. I'd love to see what you're like during the winter." Before she could utter a word, he closed the door and waved good-bye.

She laughed as she drove away, feeling pleased that he'd come along after all. Not only was he amusing, but he thought her last name was Kennedy. And bump into him? Not likely. Even if he was from Tempe, she knew the likelihood of ever seeing him was slim to none. But, she reminded herself, it wasn't as though she cared. He was a nice guy and all, but she didn't want to care about anyone else for a good long while.

Pushing all thoughts of Braxton aside, her mind began to wonder once again about Chris. *What is he doing right now? Is he enjoying his job in Oregon? Does he like Portland? Is he seeing anyone? Does he miss me? Does he ever think about me?* These questions raged through her mind, but the same old question that plagued her the most was, *why?* She missed him so much. And despite what her family and friends told her, it wasn't getting easier with time.

Small tears pooled at the corners of her eyes and slowly made their way down her cheeks. "Good grief," she spoke aloud, angrily wiping away her tears. "I am so sick of crying about you, Chris." She had tried everything to make it easier. She had tried counting up all of his faults, hoping that would provide an answer, but try as she might, she could not think of one thing wrong with him. There was not one reason why he wasn't perfect for her. Maybe *she* just wasn't good for him—maybe that was it. Yet even as the thought entered her mind, she knew she needed to stop. She needed to get her mind off him, move on, and have faith that God knew what was best for her.

❈ Chapter 2 ❈

KENNEDY RANG THE doorbell of apartment #207, waiting for a full two minutes before a girl opened the door. With a petite frame barely over five feet, she appeared to be sixteen. Light brown curly hair flew in all directions, emphasizing her youthful appearance. She appeared as though she had just woken up. "May I help you?" she asked groggily.

Kennedy assumed that the girl was a younger sister to one of her roommates. "Yes. My name is Kennedy Jackson. I'm supposed to move in here today."

Comprehension dawned in the girl's eyes. "Oh, yes, come in!" she exclaimed. She opened the door wider and waved Kennedy inside. "My name is Mia, and I'm sorry. You caught me napping, so I'm not feeling quite with it yet. I work pretty late hours, and I usually spend the day sleeping."

So this was one of her roommates. Kennedy attempted to hide her surprise. "Oh, I'm sorry for waking you," she said apologetically. "It's great to meet you, but if you could just give me my key, I will get out of your hair and let you go back to bed."

"Oh, no way!" Mia said. "I've overslept as it is, and, besides, I'm already awake." Blinking slowly, she shook her head in an effort to clear away the cobwebs of sleep. "I'll help you unload your car. In fact . . ." Her eyes lit up. "If you have a lot of stuff, I could get someone from downstairs to come and help."

"Oh, don't bother," Kennedy said, smiling. "I'm perfectly capable of unloading my own car."

"No, you don't understand!" Mia's green eyes sparkled. "I kind of have this thing for one of the guys downstairs, and this is the perfect excuse to talk to him."

Laughing, Kennedy conceded, "Okay, well, in that case I do have a lot of really heavy boxes."

"Yeah," Mia said. "No offense, but you don't look like you could lift two pounds without falling over."

"Me? And what are you supposed to be? A professional weight lifter?" Kennedy faked offense.

Giggling, Mia brought her arms down, clenched her fists, and flexed her muscles, taking on the stance of a weight lifter. "It's pretty obvious, isn't it? In fact, I've been known to have a nasty temper, so I'd try really hard to stay on my good side if I were you." Mia glanced at the clock on the wall. "I'd better hurry and call. Jerry has to leave for work in an hour."

"Oh, so he works evenings too?"

"Well, no, not usually, only this week. That's what makes liking him so stinking hard. The only day I ever see him is on Saturday." She smiled sadly as she picked up the telephone receiver. "He's obsessed with washing his car, so I can always find him out in the parking lot on his day off."

With Mia on the phone, Kennedy had some time to glance around the apartment and immediately liked what she saw. A large front room opened up to an adjoining kitchen area off to the right. A casual, deep red sectional, honey-stained coffee table, and small entertainment center holding an ancient-looking television were the only items of furniture adorning the front room. Kennedy appreciated the fact that the two rooms were uncluttered and neat. Thankfully, her new roommates didn't appear to be slobs.

The kitchen was small but tastefully colored. Light oak cupboards stretched around the kitchen, and the few things hanging on the wall accented a quaint Americana theme. Kennedy smiled in satisfaction. The apartment was homey, and Kennedy had two roommates yet to meet. She already liked Mia. A familiar warm feeling spread though her body, and she knew this was where she was supposed to be.

Mia hung up the phone, grinning like a little kid who had just found an old piece of candy under the couch cushions. "They are on their way up!" she announced.

"They? Who else is coming?"

"Oh, just Jerry's roommate, Brad," she explained matter-of-factly. Mia rushed down the hall. "I'll be right back. I have to do something with my hair before he gets here."

Only a couple of minutes passed before a knock sounded at the door. Evidently the boys downstairs didn't waste any time. Mia's voice reverberated through the apartment. "Can you get the door, Kennedy? I'll be right there."

Shaking her head and smiling to herself, Kennedy pulled the door open, coming face to face with two strangers. "Hi," she said kindly to the two guys outside. "You must be Jerry and Brad."

"Yes, ma'am." The taller of the two grinned down at her. Kennedy caught a slight Southern accent in his voice. Wow, she nearly said aloud; he was over six-and-a-half feet tall and had flaming red hair. He was not someone she would call handsome, but his friendly smile and easy nature made for a good first impression. The other guy was of average height and build and much more handsome, with blond curly hair and brown eyes. Despite his good looks, though, he appeared to be put out and not at all friendly. Hoping that Mia's little crush was on the giant rather than the grouch, Kennedy invited them inside.

The giant spoke again. "We heard there was a newcomer to the place and were told that our services were needed."

Kennedy smiled back at him. "Hi, I'm Kennedy—Mia's new roommate. It's nice to meet you." Shaking both their hands, she looked from one to the other. "So, which is which?"

The giant immediately confirmed her fears. "I'm Brad, and this here's Jerry." The grouch barely nodded in acknowledgement. He was clearly annoyed.

Kennedy's poor impression of Jerry did not improve. She made a mental note to give him the heavier boxes. "Thanks for coming up, guys. I really appreciate it."

Much to her relief, Mia finally appeared in the front room, her massive curls fastened back into a ponytail. She looked a little older with a touch of makeup, but her appearance still reflected that of an unruly child. "Hi, fellas!" Mia smiled. "Thanks for coming up!"

Jerry finally spoke as he waved in Kennedy's direction. The words came out as a drawl. "She already covered the thanks." Evidently, he was eager to do his duty and make himself scarce.

Mia didn't seem to notice his impolite tone because she laughed delightedly. "Great! Then you can times that thanks by two." Turning to Kennedy, Mia gestured toward the door. "C'mon, Kennedy, put us to work." Thankfully, the job didn't take long with the help of Brad, Jerry, and Mia. Kennedy was grateful for them—the stifling afternoon heat was nearly unbearable.

Once the car was unpacked, Mia was quick to invite Jerry and Brad to stay for some lemonade. Offering a lame excuse, Jerry made a quick retreat. Brad stayed an additional hour until Mia glanced at her wristwatch. "Oh, no!" she exclaimed. "I'd better go and get ready for work, or I'll be late!" She called a quick thanks to Brad as she rushed off down the hallway.

"Thanks for the lemonade, Mia," Brad hollered at her retreating figure. He rose from the couch and made his way to the door. Turning toward Kennedy, he smiled. "Isn't she quite the gal?"

"She sure seems to be." Kennedy smiled warmly, liking Brad more and more.

"She's lived here nearly two years now, and I don't think I've ever seen her without a smile on her face." He grinned before closing the door behind him.

As soon as he was gone, Mia came running down the hall exuberantly. "So, what did you think?"

"About what?" Kennedy evaded the question. She knew that Mia was referring to Jerry, but wasn't quite sure what to say.

"About *him*."

"Jerry or Brad?"

"Oh, who cares about Brad!" Mia exclaimed. "You know I like Jerry. So, what'd you think of him?"

Not one to lie, Kennedy asked, "Do you want my honest opinion?"

Mia's eyes clouded over, but as Brad had pointed out, she still smiled faintly. "You didn't like him." It was a statement, not a question.

"I wouldn't say that I didn't like him," Kennedy stated slowly, hating to discourage such a sweet girl.

"But?" Mia urged, her face brightening.

Losing her nerve, Kennedy bought herself some more time. "I just don't know him yet. Give me a little more time, and then I'll tell you what I think." She forced a smile to her face before declaring truthfully, "I do think he's good-looking though."

"He's gorgeous!" Mia exclaimed, glancing at her watch. "Oh! I've got to go soon. Come back and talk to me while I get ready."

"Okay." Kennedy followed Mia back to one of the bathrooms, and leaned against the doorframe, wanting to steer the subject of conversation away from Jerry. "Where do you work anyway?"

"I work at the Horizon. It's a big hotel in downtown Phoenix. I'm the front desk receptionist, and I work the night shift."

"How long have you worked there?"

"About two years—ever since I graduated from high school."

"Do you like it?"

"Not really, but it's a job and pays the bills." Mia frantically began to brush at her hair. "I plan on going to college one of these days. I've always wanted to be a kindergarten teacher."

"Really?" Kennedy asked. "That's great! You would make the perfect teacher! What's keeping you?"

"Money." Mia smiled sheepishly. "I don't want a bunch of student loans—especially on a teacher's salary—and I don't have enough money saved for school yet."

"I see." Kennedy pursed her lips in thought. "Can't you get a grant or something?"

Mia scrunched her eyebrows and applied some lip gloss to her puckered lips. "I don't know. To be honest, I've never thought about it."

"Well, I'm not sure what you're making right now, but you should easily qualify for a government grant if your parents don't claim you as a dependent."

"Really?" Mia asked, her eyes filling with excitement. "My parents pretty much told me that I was on my own once I finished high school, so I moved out and found the best job I could. Do you really think I can get a grant?"

"I think so. I'll help you look into it," promised Kennedy.

Mia squealed with delight, impulsively hugging her new roommate. "Oh thanks, Kennedy! I'm so happy you are going to live here."

✳ ✿ ✳

A half hour later, Kennedy found herself alone on the floor of her empty room, wanting to kick herself for neglecting to discover beforehand that the apartment was unfurnished. All the apartments she had lived in while attending BYU were completely furnished, so she never considered having to procure any furniture. Mia and Brad had laughed when they discovered she had no bed, and Jerry had rolled his eyes, as if disgusted with her stupidity. Sentencing herself to an uncomfortable night on the couch, Kennedy had entered her room and plopped down on the floor. She surveyed the room and wondered where to begin.

Everything was painted white, and the room had the same tan carpet that covered the floor of the front room and the rest of the apartment. Thankfully, the closet and room were decently sized. Kennedy knew that she wouldn't have too many problems fitting all her stuff into the space once she had a chest, a desk, and maybe even a small bookcase. Her boxes, luggage, and other things were all piled up just inside the bedroom door. Thinking that she should hang up her clothes before they became even more wrinkled, Kennedy simply sat there feeling the beginnings of self-pity.

With homesickness engulfing her, she couldn't help but feel alone. Her mind began to reflect back on the past year of her life and how she came to find herself in her current circumstances. Her longing for Chris was at the forefront, ruthlessly adding pain to her lonesomeness. Was her mom right? Would this ever get easier?

Kennedy closed her eyes and recalled her mother's words as they echoed through her mind. "It will get easier with time, Kennedy, but it is going to be hard for awhile. I guarantee that someday you will look back and realize it was all worth it. You are not a bitter person, and I am so proud of your attitude. I know it will be difficult, but if you can make it through without letting it make you resentful and hard, you will be much stronger for it in the end."

"I know, Mom." Kennedy sighed. "I know all that. What I don't know is how to get through it. Where do I start? How do I get rid of the hurt?"

Kennedy's mother smiled sadly. "You take it one day at a time.

You move to Tempe, start your new job, get involved in church and the community, and try your hardest to focus on other people. And of course, keep strengthening your relationship with God."

Kennedy knew the truth of her mother's words as vividly as she felt the pain of her current circumstances. Somehow, the gentle memory of the conversation gave her renewed strength. Rising from the floor, she began to rummage through the boxes in the corner until she found the one she was searching for.

She opened the box, pulled out her iPod and speakers, plugged them in, and got to work. Music always energized her and brought a smile to her face. The time flew by, and Kennedy was so immersed in organizing her belongings that she neglected to hear the arrival of her two other roommates. She was hanging up some dresses in her closet and singing at the top of her lungs when a movement in the corner of her eye made her jump.

The two girls laughed. "Sorry, we didn't mean to scare you," one of them said. "You must be Kennedy. I'm Becca, and this is Stacey." She gestured to the supermodel standing next to her. Stacey was tall, with shimmering blonde hair, blue eyes, and a perfect figure. Becca, on the other hand, was a little shorter and had curly strawberry blonde hair and freckles.

Smiling warmly, Kennedy turned down the music. "Hi. It's great to meet you both. Sorry for subjecting you to—" Kennedy paused, "—my less than flattering vocal performance."

"I don't know what you're talking about. I think your voice is remarkable," Becca said. Her green eyes crinkled with unrestrained mirth. "Stacey and I were both wondering how Gwen Stefani got into our apartment."

Kennedy smiled. "You know, for a moment I thought you were serious. In fact, I was about to recommend a good ear doctor for you. So did you both just get home from work?"

"Oh, no," Becca said. "We're just in school at Mesa Community College." She smiled impishly. "We're both snobby rich kids whose parents pay for school and everything, so we don't have to work."

"I see," Kennedy said, enjoying Becca's sense of humor. Stacey seemed a bit more subdued and private, but she was definitely friendly. "So, what are the snobby rich kids studying in school?"

"Someday, I'm going to be a famous actress." Becca sighed dramatically. "I'm studying theatre arts."

"I want to be a nurse," Stacey answered simply.

"Yep," Becca teased. "She's going to be the next Florence Nightingale, wiping the fevered brows of handsome men."

"Wow, a famous actress and a world-renowned nurse," Kennedy said. "I'm not sure if I'm qualified to live here with the two of you."

"Oh, sure you are," said Becca matter-of-factly. "With a voice like yours, you are more than qualified."

Stacey shook her head at Becca, a slight smile on her lips. "What job are you starting on Monday?" she asked.

"I'll be working for an interior design firm called Interior Essentials."

Becca's eyes lit up. "That's perfect! You can start by decorating our apartment."

Kennedy chuckled. "You are far too trusting, Becca."

"Where's your bed?" asked Stacey.

Kennedy tried to sound as serious as possible. "Oh, I don't believe in beds. A couple of years ago I went on a bush hike in the Australian outback with Crocodile Dundee. I haven't had much use for beds ever since."

Stacey looked at Kennedy in confusion, while Becca erupted in giggles.

Smiling, Kennedy explained, "Actually, I didn't realize that the apartment was unfurnished, so I'm afraid a shopping trip is in order as soon as possible. So long as you guys don't mind me sleeping on the couch tonight, I'll try to find a bed tomorrow."

"Nonsense," Becca replied. "I guarantee you won't find a furniture store within miles around that will be able to deliver a bed by tomorrow, and Stacey and I both have loads of family around with spare beds galore. With a few phone calls, we can have a bed in this room by tonight."

"Oh, no!" Kennedy argued, aghast at the thought of putting anyone to so much trouble. "I'll simply bribe a delivery boy."

"Believe us when we say that with the reputation the stores have around here," Stacey explained, "you won't be having anything delivered tomorrow. It'll be more like a week or two."

"Sorry, Kennedy," Becca bantered, "but as much as Stacey and I like you, we don't want you sleeping on our couch for that long."

Stacey's eyes suddenly brightened. "I know!" she beamed, glancing at Becca. "B. J. doesn't live far from here, and I'm sure he has to have one spare bed we can borrow. He even has a truck that he could haul it over with." Before Kennedy could dissuade her, Stacey had dashed from the room, calling over her shoulder, "I just need to make a quick phone call. Be right back!"

Kennedy shook her head, glancing at Becca with a helpless expression on her face.

"Hey, don't look at me," Becca replied. "Stacey's man is gorgeous and charming, so I wouldn't mind at all if he were to come and bring a bed over here."

"All right, fine!" Kennedy shook her head in defeat. "But I feel incredibly stupid about this."

"Think of it as a small sacrifice for your dear roomie." Becca grinned triumphantly.

"First Mia, and now Stacey," muttered Kennedy to herself. Glancing at Becca, she asked skeptically, "So, do you have a boyfriend too? If so, maybe you could give him a call and get him over here to make me some dinner."

Becca opened her mouth to comment, but Stacey sauntered back into the room.

"Well? What did he say?" Becca asked.

Stacey shrugged in disappointment. "No one answered, so I just left a message. Hopefully he'll call back soon, unless of course he's out of town on one of his business trips."

Kennedy was quick to respond. "Well, that's that then. How about this? If he doesn't call back tonight, I'll just sleep on the couch for one night, and then we'll figure out something else tomorrow—after I have tried my powers of persuasion on some unsuspecting deliveryman."

Becca and Stacey reluctantly agreed, and they watched Kennedy hang up the last of her clothes in the closet. Satisfied with the progress she had made in her bedroom, Kennedy offered a suggestion: "Well, I'm pretty much done with about all I can do in this room, so how about we go chat some more in the front room?"

Kennedy discovered that Becca and Stacey were both born and raised in Gilbert, Arizona. Their parents lived on neighboring farms, and as the East Valley rapidly expanded, they were able to sell off the majority of their land to developers and retire wealthy.

Becca did most of the talking, while Stacey seemed content to sit back and listen. Kennedy also learned that they were both sophomores at Mesa Community College and that they had been friends their entire lives. They both planned to eventually marry and set up their own homes in Arizona, living next door to each other for the rest of their lives.

In time, the topic of conversation turned to Kennedy. She answered all of their questions openly and honestly, telling them both about her beloved parents and family, as well as her years spent at BYU.

"Oh, so you're a Mormon?" Becca didn't beat around the bush.

"Yes," Kennedy replied frankly. "What about you guys?"

Becca and Stacey glanced at each other, showing some slight discomfiture at the question. It was Becca who finally answered. "Both of us were raised Catholics, but our parents weren't overly religious, so other than reading the Bible story at Christmas and attending Easter Sunday, we don't have much to do with church—but Stacey here has been taking some of those lessons the missionaries in your church offer."

"Really?" Kennedy asked, not hiding her surprise.

"Yeah," Stacey mumbled, shifting her gaze to the floor in an uneasy manner, as if not sure how to explain.

Much to Stacey's relief, Becca jumped in for the rescue. "Sorry, Stacey, but Kennedy's your roommate, and she is going to find out some time." Kennedy noticed Stacey's face turn two shades darker as Becca continued. "You see, Kennedy, Stacey's beloved B. J. is a Mormon, and she wanted to find out more about his beliefs. Plus, he always sits in on the lessons, so Stacey is able to see him more often. That's definitely a perk for her." Becca was grinning at Kennedy and didn't see the glare that Stacey directed her way.

Not wishing to cause Stacey any further discomfort, Kennedy offered an opinion of her own before Becca could continue. "That's great, Stacey. You must like B. J. a lot to want to learn more about his religion."

Stacey finally glanced up from the floor, appearing relieved and grateful. Obviously wanting the subject changed, she asked Kennedy, "So, what about you? Is there a man in your life?"

Kennedy was unprepared for the ache she felt at Stacey's innocent question. The painful throb surfaced so quickly, it took all of Kennedy's control to regain her composure. Wishing the subject away, she answered the question evasively with another question. "Does my dad count?"

Before her roommates could question her further, Kennedy jumped up from the couch and glanced at her watch. "Wow, it's getting late. Could either of you tell me where the nearest grocery store is? I want to pick up a few things before it gets any later."

Within five minutes, Kennedy had freshened up, changed into a pair of denim shorts and a yellow V-neck T-shirt, and headed out the door, grabbing her key to the apartment before she left.

❋ Chapter 3 ❋

B RAXTON TAYLOR COMPLETED the drive home from Albuquerque in no time. The company he owned was in the process of developing several subdivisions in New Mexico, and a few of their model homes were scheduled to open in one month's time. His employees were highly capable, but Braxton enjoyed overseeing the final preparation of each of his subdivisions and model homes himself. When it came to his career, he was nothing less than an over-achieving perfectionist. He enjoyed the satisfaction that came from honest, quality work, and he expected the same integrity from each of his employees.

Braxton became the CEO and President of Taylor Homes at the young age of 26, when his father, Jade Taylor, passed away. Jade originally started the company when Braxton was in his late teens, and aside from the two years Braxton spent in Australia serving an LDS mission, he worked side-by-side with his father, learning everything he could about developing and selling homes. The top executives were outraged when they learned that Taylor Homes had been left to Jade's son, and they eventually resigned from the company, therefore, leaving Braxton with the great responsibility of acting as CEO. Not willing to fail, he threw himself into the company, wanting to fulfill his father's dream of building high-quality homes for reasonable prices. Braxton immediately went through the onerous task of hiring new employees. Keeping busy, he discovered, was the best therapy for the loneliness he felt with his father—the only family he'd known for so long—gone.

Over a decade earlier, Jade had made the difficult and courageous decision to form the development firm. With an extensive background as a general contractor, he felt like he could do it on his own. It was several years of sleepless nights, disappointment, hard work, and dedication before the company finally obtained some success.

Now, years later, Braxton reflected on those difficult years with a sense of loss. The fond memories of working hard, combating potential disasters together head-on, celebrating their intermittent successes at their favorite restaurant, and occasionally leaving work early to catch a game of golf, were ones Braxton would never forget. His dad had been his best friend, and his dad's life had never been fair or easy. Not only had his dad lost his wife and two daughters, but he suffered through all the growing pains of starting a new company and died just before their first large-scale development was completed. Now, because of Jade, Taylor Homes was one of the largest, most successful developers in the western United States.

Braxton would never forget the day he received the gut-wrenching news. Devastated, he listened to the highway patrol officer explain that Jade had been involved in a fatal automobile accident. His lawyer had suggested a lawsuit against the driver at fault—a mother of two, who tragically lost one of her own in the same accident. He wished the accident had never occurred, but the last thing Braxton wanted to do was cause this woman more pain—heaven only knew how much she had suffered already. So instead of a lawsuit, he sought closure. With shaking hands, he had picked up the phone to call the woman, not remembering what was said. He only remembered that she had been tearful, remorseful, and grateful for his call. The conversation was brief, but relief and peace filled his soul as he replaced the phone. Wanting only to remember his father's smile, sense of humor, and keen wit, Braxton had tried to push the catastrophe from his mind, and move on with his life.

It was now three years later, and though Braxton still missed his father terribly, Taylor Homes eliminated much of the time he would have spent on memories. Working twice the number of hours of most of his employees left only enough time in his schedule for church. He rarely dated. Only when a good friend would beg and plead with him did he relent. The last time he'd had a serious relationship was right before his dad died. Jade hadn't liked Crystal much, but Braxton had once thought himself in love with her. That was, until his father passed away, and he saw the self-absorbed monster within her. Things ended nastily, with Crystal moving off to California in a huff to start a career in modeling. Since then, he hadn't dated anyone else more than once, and most of those dating experiences had ended in disaster. Feeling as though each of the girls were more interested in his money than in him personally, Braxton never really gave any of them a chance. He found himself burying his personal life and distancing himself from everyone—even his closest friends. It had taken him three years to find a comfort zone in his life, and now that he had found it, he intended to stay there.

Thus, it was surprising that for the first time in so many years, an image of a certain girl was preying on his mind—a proud, independent, and beautiful girl who wouldn't give him the time of day. What a refreshing change! It was preposterous, he knew, that he would feel something after such a brief encounter, but he couldn't help himself. Miss Kennedy was as adorable as she was independent, and—on top of that—she was moving to Tempe to work as an interior designer. The Fates could not have handed him a more perfect opportunity. He was well acquainted with the few prestigious firms in the Phoenix area, so with a few phone calls, he could track her down easily. Taylor Homes had their own in-house design department, but his company was in the beginning phase of constructing a new subdivision meant to cater to a more affluent market. Perhaps Miss Kennedy would be the perfect touch for the new homes. He would definitely look into the possibility.

Pulling into the parking lot of his firm, Braxton gave a self-satisfied smirk at this inspired strategy. What better way to get to know her without having to complicate matters with dating and all of its attendant pressures? It was with high spirits that he entered the building and headed for his office. When his vice president hesitantly told him that a plan to purchase a section of prime land south of Mesa had fallen through, Braxton didn't even blink an eye.

❋ ❋ ❋

Kennedy stumbled into her apartment, her arms laden with grocery bags. Evidently Becca and Stacey had gone somewhere, because the door had been locked. Grateful she had remembered her key, Kennedy dropped the groceries on the kitchen table and started to put them away before realizing how exhausted she was. Bed or no bed, she was going to get to sleep early.

As she walked to her room, she was surprised to find a note taped to her door. The elegant cursive brought good news:

Surprise! B. J. called right after you left and said that you could borrow a bed as long as you needed to. He was even kind enough to bring it right over so you would have it for tonight. Sorry we weren't here when you got home. We went to take B. J. out for ice cream. Catch you later!
Becca & Stacey

Touched by her roommates' and B. J.'s thoughtfulness, Kennedy entered her room and was startled to find the most gorgeous sleigh bed she had ever seen. The headboard and footboards were meticulously molded out of what appeared to be black walnut, stained with a rich mahogany finish. Kennedy ran her fingers over the smooth, shiny surface of the footboard, enjoying the glossy feel beneath her fingers. It looked completely out of place in her modest, diminutive room, and she couldn't believe that anyone would loan out such a beautiful bed. She had only expected a mattress. Instead, she got a bed straight out of a designer catalog.

Feeling extremely uncomfortable with being the recipient of such an extravagant loan, Kennedy made a promise to herself that she would go out first thing in the morning and not come home until she had found a store willing to deliver a bed the same day.

Kennedy yawned as she pulled her sheets and bedspread from a nearby box and quickly made up her bed. The blue and green plaid comforter with bright yellow sunflowers looked ridiculous next to the elegant bed, but after brushing her teeth, reading her scriptures, and saying her prayers, Kennedy gratefully fell asleep beneath the covers.

❋ Chapter 4 ❋

BRAXTON WAS FRUSTRATED and annoyed. He had confidently called several interior design companies he knew, as well as some he'd never heard of, and not one of them had recently employed anyone with the last name of Kennedy. He thought he was in luck when Interior Essentials told him that three new assistants were starting that very day, but when he asked to speak with a Miss Kennedy, the receptionist's squeaky voice calmly explained, "I'm sorry Mr. ah—"

"Taylor."

"Oh yes—Mr. Taylor. I'm afraid that none of the new assistants have the last name of Kennedy."

"Listen," he replied, taking a deep breath in an effort to rein in his irritation, "what about the next couple of weeks? Are any new assistants starting then?"

Once again, his optimism was dashed by the voice he was beginning to dislike intensely. "Actually, today is the beginning of our next training cycle for all the new employees," she explained. "Unless this Miss Kennedy is planning on starting work in six months' time, she would be here today. And my records only show three new individuals reporting for work today. I'm sorry to say that Miss Kennedy is not among them. I'd be more than happy to refer you to any one of our highly qualified designers, if you'd like." The receptionist oozed with false sincerity. She was as exasperated with him as he was with her.

"No, thank you." Braxton's frustration was evident as he hung up the phone. Would Miss Kennedy have lied to him about her employment? She certainly didn't seem like she was making up a story. But then again, he thought wryly, maybe she was used to getting stalked. One thing was certain—he wasn't going to give up easily.

Her job wasn't the only clue she had given him. She also mentioned that she had graduated from BYU and, therefore, was most likely a Mormon. Her move to Tempe would probably put her in one of the several university wards. Taking a deep breath, Braxton decided he would have to start attending the stake activities he had so painstakingly avoided in the past. He hoped she was more social than he was.

❈

"All new jobs are difficult at first," Kennedy told herself as she opened the door to her empty apartment. The overwhelming and mentally exhausting day had taken its toll, and Kennedy wanted nothing more than to crawl into bed with a good book.

Marching straight to her room, Kennedy removed her cream linen vest and placed it on a hanger in the closet. She kicked off her matching pumps and glanced at herself in the floor-length mirror hung on the back of her closet. Of all the clothes she had purchased for her new job, the ensemble she was wearing was by far her favorite. Watching her reflection in the mirror, Kennedy knew that she looked her best. So why had she spent the entire day feeling like a self-conscious clod who couldn't utter a coherent sentence? She hoped her second day would be better.

Slowly, she changed from her pantsuit into some comfortable khaki shorts and a white V-neck shirt. She had been planning to go to family home evening in her new ward, but, in her current mood, the last thing she wanted to do was socialize.

Wandering into the kitchen, Kennedy checked the messages before opening the refrigerator. She'd been hoping to hear back from the idiotic furniture company and was disappointed to find only messages for Becca and Stacey. She thought her prayers had been answered on Saturday when she finally tracked down a quaint little furnishings store. It didn't take her long to find the perfect country bedroom set. It was made of pine and was stained in a natural finish, and it included a bed, a chest of drawers, and a desk. The store employee assured her that it would be no problem to deliver the furniture later that same day.

It wasn't until that evening that the store called with bad news: The chest and desk would be delivered shortly, but the bed was out of stock, and, because they were expecting a new shipment the following week, they were unable to give her the one on display. Much to her aggravation, Kennedy was forced to continue to borrow B. J.'s bed, with no idea when her own would be delivered.

Pulling a jar of applesauce from the refrigerator, Kennedy grabbed a spoon from the drawer and seated herself at the kitchen table, spooning the applesauce into her mouth directly from the jar. Her mother would have been mortified if she were there. The thought made Kennedy smile.

As if on cue, her cell phone rang, startling her into dropping a spoonful of applesauce down the front of her shirt. "Oh, blast!" she exclaimed as she grabbed the phone. "Hello?" With the phone held securely between her ear and her shoulder, Kennedy advanced to the sink, grabbed a rag, and attempted to remove the applesauce stain.

"Hi, sweetheart," a wonderfully familiar voice said from the other end of the line.

"Mom?" Kennedy asked excitedly.

"I was just calling to see how your first day of work went."

Groaning, Kennedy rolled her eyes. "Let's just say that it's typical for your first day of work to go badly."

"Pretty overwhelming, huh?" Olivia asked.

"To say the least," Kennedy replied, "I think everything that could possibly have gone wrong did. First of all, I was late to work. I underestimated the traffic. Also, I seemed to drop just about everything I touched and trip over any inanimate object in sight. And to make matters worse, my supervisor, Shauna, who seemed so kind and gracious throughout all of our interviews, is actually a grizzly bear trapped inside a human body. Every suggestion or opinion I expressed was met with, and I quote, 'Now dear, don't forget who you're working for. We are the most prestigious design firm in the state, and we need to reflect a great deal of professionalism in our work.'

"I felt like a complete idiot the entire day. My confidence in any ability I thought I had is now shattered. Mom, Shauna has seen my portfolio and my work. Why in the world did she hire me if she doesn't agree with my sense of style and design?" Kennedy let out an irritated sigh.

"Well, I can't explain Shauna's actions, but I do know that she wouldn't have hired you if she didn't think you were talented. Try not to judge her prematurely. Maybe she had a terrible weekend or a colleague belittled her work recently or something. You never know. One thing is certain, though. You can't let this woman tear down your own self-confidence in your work. You were top of your class at school, and you know that all of your professors were very excited about your ideas and your projects.

"But you do need to remember that you are an assistant right now. You are there to learn as much as you can from Shauna. I'm sure that if you treat her with respect, she will eventually offer the same respect back to you. Give her time. One day she will utilize the great talent in you that so many others have already seen."

"Mom, you always know the perfect thing to say. I hope you're right. Thank you." Kennedy smiled, feeling a little better. "So what's going on with you? I want to hear about you and Dad and the family. How is everyone?"

"Oh, fine, as usual. I'm afraid I don't have any earth-shattering news to tell." Her mother casually switched the subject back to Kennedy. "So, it's Monday. What's on your agenda for tonight? Is your ward having family home evening tonight?"

"Yeah, but I don't really feel like going. I'm not exactly in what you'd call a socializing mood."

"Too bad. I bet you'd have fun. It would get your mind off your terrible day."

"Or add to it," joked Kennedy.

"I suppose that's the chance you have to take," Olivia bantered back. "Besides, maybe you'll meet a rich and charming frog you can take home and keep until you are ready to kiss him and change him into your prince."

Chuckling, Kennedy shook her head at her mother's words. "Mom, do you realize how bizarre you are sometimes?"

"Yeah, and guess who's got my genes?"

"Oh, geez, you're right. I'm doomed," said Kennedy.

Olivia laughed outright. "So are you going to FHE or not?"

"I suppose I don't have much choice in the matter. Not if I'm to meet my future amphibious prince."

"Terrific!" Olivia exclaimed. "Then I will let you go so you can get ready, and I'll call you later on this week to see if that job of yours improves."

"Thanks, Mom," Kennedy replied. "I'll talk to you later."

✳ ❊ ✳

Jillian, the Relief Society president in Kennedy's new ward, immediately took Kennedy under her wing when she arrived at the park for family home evening. The ward was just about to start a game of capture the flag using water guns. It promised to be a fun, wet evening, and Kennedy was grateful to be out of her apartment.

"Kennedy, I want you to meet my brother, Jason," Jillian said.

Following her gaze, Kennedy saw a tall, lanky man with wavy brown hair, crinkled green eyes, and a gigantic smile. Kennedy couldn't help but think he looked like Jimmy Stewart in his twenties. He was quite a contrast to his short, stout younger sister, but they both had the same cheerful expressions. Liking the siblings immediately, Kennedy extended her hand and smiled as she greeted him. "Hi, Jason, it's nice to meet you." Quirking her eyebrows, she couldn't help but ask, "Have you ever played the lead in *It's a Wonderful Life*?"

Jason laughed, his smile growing even larger. "You see the resemblance too, do you? Maybe I can reenact one of the scenes for the ward talent show coming up." He leaned in conspiringly. "So, tell me, have you met the entire ward yet? I have to warn you that once my sister starts the introduction process, it doesn't end until you've met everyone and remember no one."

Jillian slugged her brother. "He's only hoping you'll remember his name. He never forgets a name, and it annoys him beyond belief when someone forgets his."

Kennedy laughed before Jason had a chance to defend himself. "Well, if that was your objective, Jason, it worked. I promise to never forget your name."

"Ah ha!" Jason nudged his sister with his elbow, grinning like a boy who had just won his first pinewood derby contest. "You see, sis? It worked! I'll be sure to use that line on every newcomer from now on."

Before their conversation could continue, the bishop called the group to attention. "Okay, everyone, come gather over here so we can divide you into teams, explain the rules, and get this game started!" The ward was efficiently divided into two teams with Jillian and Kennedy on team one and Jason on team two.

"Now," the bishop continued, "we've divided the park in half—with an imaginary line between those two large ash trees." He gestured in the direction of the trees. "Team number one will be on the north side, and team number two will take the south. The object of the game is to capture the opposing side's flag without getting caught and placed in their prison. If you do get put in prison, someone from your own team will have to come and tag you to get you out. Because we're playing with water guns, each of you will tag the opposing members or your own teammates by spraying them with water." The bishop glanced through the crowd, making sure everyone understood. Once he was assured, he bellowed, "Let the game begin!"

To make the game even more interesting, the FHE leaders had sprayed the area down with water beforehand, creating a slippery playing field. Within minutes, the entire ward was soaked and covered in grass stains. Kennedy was now grateful for the applesauce stain that prompted her to change into a black T-shirt. She was also thankful that she had come. Chasing down complete strangers and dousing them with water couldn't have been more therapeutic. She forgot all about work and Chris and simply enjoyed herself.

Unlocking her car to return home, Kennedy heard a familiar voice shout across the parking lot, "Hey, Kennedy, do you remember my name?"

Looking at Jason, dripping wet and wearing a broad smile, Kennedy yelled back, "Yeah, it's Jimmy, right?"

"You better believe it!"

✿ Chapter 5 ✿

"WHAT A WEEK!" Braxton raked his fingers through his hair as he blinked at his monitor. It was Friday evening, and he was still in his office, feeling completely exhausted. He had a few reports to punch out before his meeting Monday morning, but they would have to wait until tomorrow. Glancing at his watch, he quickly shut down his computer and rose, stretching his arms as he yawned.

There was a stake social that night, and though he had no desire to attend when he was in need of a good night's rest, the anticipation that he might encounter Miss Kennedy propelled him out to his truck and on home to shower and change. Besides, he tried to convince himself, even if she wasn't in attendance, his appearance might appease his bishopric and get them off his back for a while. Their nagging at him to be more social was becoming more pronounced. At age twenty-nine, he was already feeling a little too old for the ward—especially this time of year when so many new freshmen were starting school and showing up at church.

Pulling into his neighborhood, Braxton rounded the corner and headed for his home at the end of the cul-de-sac. The sun was going down, but he was able to clearly see the home he had built a year earlier. It had taken him months to find the lot, which was located in a quaint little neighborhood. The tree-lined streets, green lawns, and unusual brick homes had immediately attracted his attention and provided a distinctly unique feel from so many of the other neighborhoods he had perused. He'd had to purchase two lots in order to procure the acre of land he now owned. Though it was fairly pricey, he fell in love with the property on sight and immediately set to work drawing up plans for his home.

Unlike most of the houses in Arizona, the exterior was built with solid brick rather than stucco. Another unique characteristic he was adamant about including was a basement. With the relentless heat Arizona so abundantly provided, a basement only made sense. Therefore, he built a large ranch-style home with a basement, five bedrooms, five bathrooms, an office, a game room, an exercise room, and a four-car garage. Many people had thought him senseless for building such an extravagantly sized home, but he planned on eventually raising his family there.

Braxton pulled into his garage and entered his empty home. His footsteps echoed off the hardwood floor and through the hallway as he made his way to the kitchen. With ten-foot ceilings, his home appeared even larger. The hardwood floor extended into the kitchen and accentuated the lofty maple cabinets. A large island was situated to separate the kitchen from the extensive family room. With a great view to the backyard, the window-lined family room was by far his favorite room. He particularly enjoyed his big-screen plasma television and comfortable recliner.

Checking the telephone messages, Braxton wasn't surprised to hear from his home teacher, reminding him about the stake activity that night. The next message was from one of the few childhood friends he had left. "Hey, B. J., this is Stacey. Sorry to bother you again, but I just wanted you to know that my new roommate finally had her bed delivered, so you can come and pick up yours whenever you'd like. We'll be around for the next few hours, if that works for you. Just let me know. Thanks again! I'll talk to you later."

It wasn't exactly convenient, especially when the stake activity was starting soon, but Braxton also knew that this new roommate was not going to enjoy having an additional bed take up space in the apartment. Deciding that he could go to the activity a little late, Braxton sighed as he picked up the phone. Besides, he could always invite Stacey and her roommates to the social. She seemed to be getting more and more serious about the gospel, so perhaps she'd like to go, meet new people, and see what an activity was like.

❋ ❋ ❋

"Yes!" Stacey shrieked as she hung up the phone. Surprised, Becca and Kennedy glanced up from their positions on the couch, waiting expectantly for Stacey to explain her unusual outburst. She didn't disappoint them. "B. J. is on his way over to pick up the bed. He also invited us to go to some steak party with him." Stacey looked apologetically toward Kennedy. "I'm sorry we won't be able to go with you to your church shindig. Would you like to come with us instead?"

Before Kennedy could respond, Becca's eyebrow rose in question. "What's a steak party?"

Pursing her lips in thought, Stacey shrugged her shoulders. "I don't know. He probably meant a steak barbecue or something with some of his friends."

"Oh?" Becca's interest was suddenly piqued. "Some of his friends, huh? I could handle that." She grinned from ear to ear.

Listening to their exchange, Kennedy could contain her mirth no longer. Becca and Stacey stared at her in bewilderment.

"What are you laughing about?" Becca asked, completely confused. "Don't you want to go meet cute, eligible men and eat yummy steak?"

Giggles turned into uncontrolled laughter as Kennedy nearly fell off the couch, holding her aching abdomen. It took her several minutes to calm down enough to explain. "B. J. has misinformed you, Stacey. The 'steak party' he was talking about is the same church activity I was just inviting you to. In Mormon lingo, the word *stake* really means a conglomeration of several wards, not good meat." Kennedy wiped the tears from her eyes, and she continued, "But don't worry, I'm sure they will be serving some sort of refreshments."

"Oh." Becca didn't try to hide her disappointment.

"Becca, don't worry." Kennedy tried to cheer up her roommate. "There are bound to be hosts of eligible bachelors for you to meet."

Stacey still looked perplexed. "Are you sure, Kennedy?"

"Yeah, I'm sure."

"Well then, I guess we won't have to try and convince you to ditch your party for ours anymore, huh? Not if it's the same one."

Kennedy grinned. "I would love to go with you guys."

"Great!" Stacey exclaimed. "Then it's all settled." Grabbing Becca by the hand, Stacey pulled her up from the couch. "C'mon, Becca, let's go get ready. B. J. will be here in half an hour."

"Oh, all right then," Becca mumbled as the two girls rushed off down the hallway.

Kennedy had already changed and was ready to go. Trying to think of something to do, she decided that she could whip up some cookies for B. J. to say thanks for loaning her the bed. Pulling her recipe box from the cupboard, Kennedy grabbed a bowl and scanned the recipe.

Once most of the ingredients were added to the mixing bowl, Kennedy searched around the kitchen for what her roommates called the community flour. They had all agreed to share the baking supplies and then take turns refilling the containers when they were empty.

After searching through every cupboard without locating the flour, she spotted the container on the top of one of the cupboards. She smiled in satisfaction as she reached for the flour. Standing on her tiptoes, Kennedy was slowly able to work the container to the edge of the cupboard. Just as the weight shifted and the flour container tilted down toward her, a thunderous, ill-timed knock sounded at the door. Startled, Kennedy let go of the container. She shrieked as it came careening down, smacked her squarely on the skull, and spilled flour everywhere.

The person responsible for her situation heard the shout and immediately let himself in, finding an aggravated girl covered in fine white dust. Becca and Stacey also came barreling into the kitchen, their hair still in curlers. Becca took in Kennedy's appearance and raised her hand to her mouth in an effort to smother her laughter. "What in the world happened to you?"

Wiping the flour from her eyes, Kennedy finally managed to open them and look at the small gathering staring in her direction, trying hard not to laugh. Taking on a dignified expression, Kennedy explained, "Well, I missed Utah so much that I decided to pretend it was snowing." She began brushing the flour off her arms and shirt. "Not that I particularly wanted to be a snowman." Glancing at the three faces, she continued, "What? Have none of you ever seen snow before?"

Braxton, Becca, and Stacey all burst into laughter, obviously thinking the situation quite hilarious. Not as amused, Kennedy glared at the three people laughing at her expense. Her gaze rested on the newcomer. Recognizing a familiar face, yet not remembering where she knew him from, she questioned him. "Do I know you? You look familiar."

Braxton let his laughter die as he glanced back in Kennedy's direction. "I don't think so," he said slowly, a smile tugging at the corners of his mouth. "I think I would have remembered meeting a snowman."

Rolling her eyes, Kennedy ignored his comment and her room-mates' laughter, abruptly remembering where she'd seen him before. "No, you're wrong," she said matter-of-factly. "Maybe you don't remember, but we have met. On the road somewhere between here and New Mexico, remember?" Searching his face, she gave an additional clue. "You helped me change my tire."

Comprehension and surprise etched across his face. "Miss Kennedy?" He couldn't believe his luck. All this time, she had been the one borrowing his bed.

"Miss Kennedy?" Becca finally piped up, looking at Braxton strangely. "Since when did you become so proper?"

"When I don't know her first name."

Before Kennedy could say a word, Becca responded, "But her first name *is* Kennedy. Kennedy Jackson."

"Really?" Braxton didn't suppress his astonishment. "Well, no wonder—" He caught himself before revealing that he had been trying to track her down.

Kennedy was surprised that he even remembered her name at all. Feeling like an idiot, all she could think to say was, "I'm sorry I don't remember your name, but I'm sure you didn't introduce your-self as B. J. It was something different."

"Braxton Jade Taylor," he clarified, glancing at Stacey. "Curly Sue over here just uses my childhood nickname because she's known me forever."

Suddenly, Stacey remembered the curlers in her hair. Her hands flew to her head in a self-conscious manner. Pulling Becca with her, she said hastily, "We'll go finish getting ready now, if that's all right with you."

"Sure," Braxton was quick to say. "I'll just help Kennedy clean up this mess and then take the bed back to my house. That should give you all enough time to get ready." He smiled pointedly at Kennedy.

"You know, if it wasn't for you, I wouldn't be looking like an albino in the first place."

"Me? I don't recall dumping the flour on you.'

"If you hadn't pounded on the door and scared me, I wouldn't have dropped the flour on myself. A simple rap on the door would have sufficed."

"Not if all of you were back in your rooms getting ready, like I figured you'd be." He grinned, his dimples forming on the edge of his mouth.

"Not all girls take forever to get ready," she sparred back.

"Oh, great, we're getting back to the chauvinist issue again, aren't we?" He laughed. Kennedy did not smile back. "I really am sorry, Kennedy," he offered, "but you have to admit, it is pretty funny."

Kennedy reached down to pick up the container with the remaining flour in it and walked toward Braxton with a wicked gleam in her eye. "I wonder. Would you think it was so funny if you were covered too?"

Braxton stood his ground, smiling confidently. "I would be laughing my head off," he answered smugly, certain she wouldn't dare.

"Well you better start laughing," Kennedy responded with sugarcoated sweetness. Then she dumped the remaining contents over Braxton's head.

"What the heck?" he spluttered, completely caught off guard.

"You're not laughing," Kennedy said, sounding anything but contrite.

Braxton wiped his face and brushed the flour off his hair and clothes the best he could. "I suppose this is the thanks I get for helping you change a tire and loaning you a bed."

"Touché," Kennedy said, chuckling. "Listen, I really am sorry. Sometimes, I can be a little rash."

"There's a shocker." He inclined his head, brushing flour from it as he did so. "Now, how about you go and get ready while I clean up this mess and take the bed back?"

"No way," came her quick reply. "I was partly responsible, so I'll clean it up myself. You go take the bed back and change. By the time you return, I promise to have myself and the kitchen all spick-and-span."

"I can't believe we are arguing over cleaning," he muttered as he grabbed a broom from the closet and tossed the dustpan in her direction.

✳ ❀ ✳

Braxton was marginally more excited to go to the stake activity, considering he was now going with Kennedy rather than simply hoping she would attend. There were a million other things he would prefer to do in the company of Kennedy Jackson, but he wouldn't complain. He smiled to himself as he steered his truck into the lot of a nearby park.

The four of them had to literally jump from the shiny black Silverado since it was jacked up several inches. Kennedy heard someone call her name as they started toward the pavilions. Spinning around toward the direction of the voice, she saw Jason waving and walking quickly toward her. "Hey! How's it going, Kennedy?" Jason grinned as he jovially clapped an arm around her shoulder. "I'm glad you made it!"

Kennedy's smile broadened at the sight of a familiar face. "Well, if it isn't Jimmy Stewart!" Jason laughed while Braxton, Becca, and Stacey looked on questioningly.

"Oh, come on," Kennedy said to Stacey and Becca, pointing at Jason. "Surely you see the resemblance. He could be Jimmy Stewart's clone."

Becca squinted. "You are so right!" She looked expectantly at Jason. "How are you at impersonations?"

Kennedy cut in quickly, "Never mind her, Jason. She's a drama major." She quickly made the introductions, and Jason invited them all to join his group. "We've been here for a while, so we've got the best seats." Jason beamed as he led them all over to the pavilions, gesturing toward a table. "Completely shaded and right next to the food!"

Becca laughed, while the others just smiled. Leaning toward Kennedy, she whispered, "Now there's one guy I would love to get to know. He's cute!"

"I know," Kennedy said quietly with a mischievous smile. "And if you come to church with me on Sunday, you'll get to see him again."

"You know, it just might be worth it." Becca's eyes twinkled in response as they arrived at a table filled with a very hungry crowd. Just as the introductions were complete, dinner started, and they all lined up to pile their plates high with food.

"Braxton Taylor?" a female voice nearly shouted. "Is that you?" All talk died at the table as each person turned to stare toward the speaker.

Cringing subtly at the familiar voice, Braxton gradually followed suit and glanced up. Pasting a pleased look on his face, he gave what he hoped sounded like an appropriate response. "Crystal! What are you doing here?" Braxton placed his fork back on the table as he slowly stood to face the girl.

"I just got back to town," Crystal responded. Crystal was a tall, exotic-looking woman with long, black hair, dark-brown eyes, and an olive complexion—she was beyond beautiful. Her slim figure sported a white, trendy, laced-up shirt and some snug-fitting jeans. She looked like she had stepped straight off the cover of *Vogue* magazine.

Kennedy took in the newcomer's appearance with mild curiosity, wondering what it was about the girl that made her look so out of place. She glanced toward Stacey to ask if she knew the identity of this stranger but stopped mid-thought when she noted the complete hatred written across Stacey's face. Kennedy didn't think it was possible, but the look only worsened as she watched Braxton take Crystal's arm and steer her away from the curious crowd.

Looking instead to Becca, Kennedy immediately noticed the worried expression on her face. Kennedy got Becca's attention and raised her eyebrows in silent questioning. Immediately, Becca snapped to attention. "Well, who wants some dessert?" She stared meaningfully at Kennedy.

"You can count me in," Kennedy piped up. She grimaced as she looked at her plate, which was still filled with food. "What about you, Stace?"

Stacey was only half listening as she mumbled, "No, thanks, I'm full."

"All right then, we'll be back in a sec." Becca pulled Kennedy's arm and led her over to the dessert table.

"Okay, Kenn, I'm going to make this quick, before Stacey comes out of her trance," Becca said as she dished a heaping spoonful of ice cream into her Styrofoam bowl. "Her name is Crystal Beckwith. She's B. J.'s former girlfriend from years ago. Basically, the girl is a jerk. She is all take and no give, if you know what I mean. When B. J.'s father died—"

"Braxton's father died?" Kennedy cut in.

"Long story, I'll tell you later." Becca was talking faster by the second. "Like I was saying, when his father died, he naturally went through a really rough time, and instead of helping him through it, she high-tailed it out of here and moved to California where she was hoping to start a modeling career. B. J. never heard from her again, at least not that I know of—until today."

"Wow," said Kennedy. "No wonder Stacey looked like she was about to strangle the girl."

"Yeah, but you didn't hear it from me," Becca said abruptly as she walked back to join her miserable roommate at the table.

An hour later, Braxton still hadn't returned, and Stacey was definitely not having fun. Getting fed up with attempting to divert her non-distractible friend, Becca directed a pleading look toward Kennedy, who was in the middle of a conversation with Jason. Catching Becca's look from the corner of her eye, Kennedy politely waited for a convenient time to change the subject. "Jason, I'm not usually the type to ask favors, but I have a big one for you."

"Shoot."

"Well, Stacey isn't feeling so great, probably just a headache or something, and Braxton seems to have disappeared for who knows how long, so would you mind giving us a ride home?"

"Gee, I'd love to, but I'm afraid I'm on the stake activity committee, and I promised to stay and help clean up." Jason nodded his head in the direction of the food tables, which were starting to be picked up. "But I can take you when I'm done."

Feeling desperate, Kennedy spoke quickly. "How about an exchange then? I'll stay and clean up for you if you take Becca and Stacey home for me."

Waving off Kennedy's suggestion like it was the nuttiest thing he'd heard all night, Jason shook his head. "Don't be crazy. I couldn't leave you to clean up. How would you get home?"

Kennedy thought quickly. "I'll either wait for Braxton or catch a ride with someone else," she reasoned. "I'm positive there is someone here wanting to do a charitable act." She grabbed Jason's arm to stop the argument forming on the tip of his tongue. "And I wouldn't mind staying at all. It would give me the opportunity to meet some new people. Please, Jason. I would really appreciate it."

Noting the determined look in her eye, Jason finally nodded. "Fine. But not until I make sure you have another ride home." He left to speak to some of his fellow committee members while Kennedy made her way to Stacey and Becca.

"Hey, I've got good news." Kennedy sat down next to Stacey and put her arm around her. "Jason is on his way home, and he'd be happy to take you guys if you'd like."

"We'd love to," Becca gushed before Stacey could argue. "But aren't you coming with us?"

"I agreed to help clean up, so I'll be home a little later." Kennedy nodded her head toward Jason, who was now approaching. "He's already found me a ride home, so don't worry."

"Kennedy." Jason pointed at a short, freckled-faced redhead who was waving back at them. "That's Rick. He's going in your direction and said you could catch a ride with him."

"Thanks, Jason." Kennedy smiled appreciatively.

"No problemo." Jason offered each of his arms to Stacey and Becca. "Now, if you don't mind, I have two beautiful ladies to see home." Becca grinned broadly while Stacey gave him a tentative smile, as the two girls grabbed each of his arms. "As for you." He pointed suavely at Kennedy. "We'll catch your act later."

Kennedy waved them off and made her way over to help clean up. There were five in all who stayed, and in a short hour they had mostly finished. Kennedy was carrying the last box of food to Rick's car when she heard her name. Turning her head, she found Braxton pacing quickly across the parking lot toward her.

"Well, if it isn't Braxton Taylor!" She loaded the box in the trunk, smiled, and turned to face him.

He looked sheepish. "Ah, sorry about that," he mumbled. He looked around at the near-empty pavilion. "Looks like I missed all the fun."

"Oh, don't worry." Kennedy shrugged her shoulders. "You really didn't miss much. It was mainly a get-to-know-you night for new people like me." She started walking back toward the pavilion. Braxton fell into step beside her. "Besides, from all the gossip floating around about how you never go to these things anyway, I'm sure you didn't miss anything," she said innocently, directing a side-long glance at Braxton.

He knew too well about his reputation, and normally he wouldn't care, but somehow Kennedy managed to make him feel slightly bad for his lax attitude. "Guilty as charged, I guess," he conceded before changing the subject. "Where are Stacey and Becca?"

"Stacey wasn't feeling so great, so they left a little early."

Braxton could have kicked himself. Here he was the ward mission leader, and he couldn't even manage to properly introduce Stacey and Becca. And to make matters worse, he left them with Kennedy, a newcomer herself, to fend for them, as well as find her roommates a ride home. If only Crystal hadn't shown up and ruined everything.

Noticing the worried expression on Braxton's face, Kennedy tried to make him feel better. "Relax, Brax." She smiled at her rhyme. "Everything worked out fine. Stacey and Becca had a great time," she fibbed, "and I got to fulfill my compassionate service requirement for the month and meet some fun, new people."

He allowed himself a slight smile. "Compassionate service requirement?" he echoed.

"Sure," Kennedy said as they approached Rick and the other members of the committee. "One hour tops each month."

Braxton chuckled, and Kennedy introduced him to a couple of the people on the committee that he had never met before. Rick happened to be in Braxton's ward, so the two knew each other pretty well.

"Ready to go, Kennedy?" Rick asked as he picked up the last box of decorations.

"Sure am," she replied, before explaining to Braxton. "Rick offered to drive me home because I wasn't sure when you'd be coming back."

Not wanting to let an opportunity pass to be alone with Kennedy, he turned to Rick. "I can take her home. I need to go by her apartment anyway and talk to Stacey about finalizing a time for the last discussion tomorrow with the missionaries."

"Okay then," Rick said. "Thanks so much for your help, and I guess I'll see you around."

Kennedy waved good-bye and turned to Braxton. "Ready to go?"

"Yeah, but I do have a huge favor to ask you."

"Okay," she said, "but just remember that I've already fulfilled my service requirement, so if it's anything big, it'll have to wait until next month."

"Thanks for the reminder," Braxton said. "The thing is, I didn't get to finish my dinner, and I'm starving. Would you mind stopping with me somewhere on the way so I can get my stomach to stop growling?"

"Only if you buy me a chocolate shake." Kennedy grinned mischievously.

"Didn't you just eat?" Braxton teased.

"Yes, but doing all the cleanup made me hungry again."

❋ ✿ ❋

"So, are you going to be cooperative and tell me, or do I have to ask?" Kennedy never could keep curiosity from getting the better of her. She and Braxton were sitting in an In-N-Out Burger waiting for their order.

"Tell you what?"

Rolling her eyes, Kennedy continued determinedly. "About your former girlfriend."

He was in mid-swallow when she asked the question. It caught him so off-guard that he inhaled, rather than swallowed, the remaining water in his mouth and started to cough. "Come again?" he spluttered between coughs.

Kennedy smiled at the uncomfortable look on his face. Undeterred, she leaned across the table and smiled sweetly. "Remember all the questions you pelted at me on the highway? Now it's your turn. Are you going to tell me willingly, or do we have to play it again?"

"Hey, I'd be more than happy to tell you where I work and what city I live in. I'd even tell you my speeding ticket history. But I did not ask you about any past boyfriends, so this is completely different." Braxton shook his head at Kennedy's audacity. This was the last subject in the world he would ever want to discuss with her. He could have kissed the fast-food worker when their number was called. "Be right back!" He jumped from the booth and went to collect their food.

He returned a moment later with Kennedy's shake and a double-double burger and fries for him.

"So, how many tickets have you had?"

"Tickets?"

"For speeding," she reminded.

"Oh," he chuckled. "Are we talking only about the ones still on my record?"

"No."

"Okay then." He did a quick mental count. "That would have to be fourteen, then—no wait, fifteen, if you count my trip to Hawaii."

Kennedy's eyes widened. "Are you kidding me?"

"I like to drive fast."

"I can't believe you still have your license."

"I did lose it for awhile as a teenager, but now I'm more careful. Having a radar detector has helped." He grinned wickedly across the table.

"Remind me not to drive with you anymore." Kennedy picked up her shake and decided to change the subject. "So, when did you first meet Crystal?"

Rolling his eyes, he decided he'd have to answer sooner or later.

But that didn't mean he would have to give her too many details. "In a class."

"Which one?"

"Scuba diving."

"Really? How fun!"

"Yeah, it was."

Kennedy grinned. "So, was it love at first sight then? She is gorgeous."

He ignored her question and continued to gulp down his burger and fries. He was suddenly in a hurry to get her home.

Watching him squirm, Kennedy decided to back off. She laid her hand on his arm saying quietly, "Hey listen, I'm only teasing you. Even you have to admit that it got a little uncomfortable at the activity." She removed her arm and rested her head on the back of the booth. "But I am intensely curious about Crystal now." She gave him a sly grin before continuing. "I partly wanted to get you back for the harassment you gave me on the highway."

Feeling much better, Braxton grinned. "Don't worry. You definitely held your own." Then, not knowing why, he suddenly felt a crazy desire to tell Kennedy everything. Tell her about Crystal and his dad. Tell her about the difficult years he had put behind him. Everything. For some reason, he felt as though he could finally open up to someone. But she was practically a stranger.

Braxton shook his head to clear the thoughts racing through his mind. He couldn't share his whole life story with this girl. Finishing up the last of his drink, he glanced at Kennedy, who was watching him with a perplexed look on her face. Smiling, he only said, "So, you seem to be handling the heat better. Your temperament has definitely improved."

"Most likely because cooler weather is just around the corner," she replied candidly. "Come spring, I would definitely steer clear of me."

He nodded in understanding. "How did you like Utah?"

"Loved it," she said. "Growing up in New Mexico, we saw snow a handful of times, but it never stuck. It was so much fun to actually go sledding and build a snowman. I even tried my hand at skiing a few times. I was terrible, but it was fun."

"I prefer snowboarding myself." He chuckled at the surprised look on her face. "Arizona does have some ski resorts, you know."

She laughed. "Well, maybe I'll give it another try then."

"Let me know when you want to, and we can go up together. I know the resorts here like the back of my hand."

"That would be great," she said. "Does Stacey ski?"

"Nope. She's never cared to learn."

"Well, maybe we can convince her to go as well."

"Sure." He munched some of his french fries and wondered why Kennedy would want to bring Stacey. It was never much fun to go skiing with someone who had never been before. Shoving the last fry into his mouth, he asked, "Ready to go?"

Kennedy only nodded, following him out of the restaurant. As he opened the car door for her, she smiled. "Thanks for the shake."

"Anytime." He closed the door, realizing that he actually meant it.

❂ Chapter 6 ❂

Some weeks later, Kennedy was determined to fulfill her promise to Mia and find some financial aid information on school grants. Her computer had broken down earlier in the day, and so she offered to fill in while the receptionist went to lunch. Between phone calls, it didn't take long for Kennedy to find the right forms on the Internet and print them out. The last page was printing when the phone rang.

Kennedy grabbed the receiver. "Hi, you have reached Interior Essentials. May I help you?"

"Yeah." The deep voice sounded vaguely familiar. "May I please speak with Kennedy Jackson?"

Surprised, yet unable to put a face with the name, Kennedy said quickly, "This is she. May I help you?"

"Kennedy? Do you normally answer the phone?"

Racking her brain for any hint as to who might be on the line, she wasn't quite sure what do say. Was this a casual call or a professional call? She opted to keep it on a more professional level. Better to be safe than sorry. "I'm just filling in for the receptionist for an hour or so. Was there something you needed?" she asked politely.

"Yeah, I wanted to talk to you about getting together a proposal for some of my new homes going up."

Who is this? Kennedy wanted desperately to ask, but instead she continued to pretend she knew exactly who she was speaking with, praying that she would have an epiphany and remember. "Okay. We will need a copy of the floor plans and a general idea of the style you want to go with. It would also be a good idea to set up a time to meet with you." Shauna had taught her a little about what was needed from a potential client.

"Sounds great," the voice responded. "How's tomorrow for lunch?"

"Fine." Kennedy was dying. "But as you probably know, I'm just an assistant, so I'll need to check with my supervisor to see if tomorrow will work for her as well." Who was this guy?

"Fine. We could go to a nice little Chinese restaurant I know out in your neck of the woods." He sounded like he was in a hurry. "I can pick you both up if you'd like."

Oh geez, now what? Not wanting to be picked up by a stranger, Kennedy said quickly, "How about we just meet you there?"

"Well . . . okay. If that works best for you. Now if your supervisor can't make it tomorrow, give me a call." He swiftly gave her directions to the restaurant as well as his number. Before Kennedy could speak another word, he said good-bye and hung up the phone. What in the world? How was she supposed to know who she was having lunch with tomorrow? And who was he anyway? Did he have the right person? Did he mean to meet with someone else? Kennedy was berating herself for not having the guts to ask for his name. This was just fabulous. Now she was stuck. And the worst part about it was that she had to tell Shauna what had happened. She could already imagine the look on Shauna's face when Kennedy told her that she had set up a lunch meeting with an anonymous man. Sighing, Kennedy accepted the fact that she would be giving Shauna yet another excuse to think her inept.

The receptionist arrived back from lunch, and Kennedy made her way upstairs with trepidation. Knocking softly on her supervisor's office door, Kennedy stepped inside when she heard a brusque, "Enter!"

"Yes?" Shauna asked with raised eyebrows.

Kennedy quickly explained the situation and watched Shauna's eyebrows rise considerably higher on her forehead. "You mean to tell me that you made a lunch appointment for us without asking me and without knowing who you were making it with?"

Kennedy knew she was in the wrong, but she refused to cower before Shauna. "Yes, that appears to be the case." Seating herself in a comfortable chair opposite Shauna, Kennedy continued. "Listen,

Shauna, I am sincerely sorry. But to be honest, he didn't let me get a word in edgewise. Evidently he was in a big hurry and for some reason assumed I knew who he was. At any rate, what's done is done, and if you can't make it, I suppose that I'll call the man back, find out who he is, and tell him we'll have to reschedule."

Shauna closed her eyes, slightly shaking her head from side to side, as if she couldn't believe what she was hearing. "He said he needed some model homes decorated?"

"Yes."

"Then I suppose I'll have to cancel my meeting tomorrow for this unexpected lunch." Shauna's voice held a subtle edge.

Being properly gracious, Kennedy replied, "Thank you, Shauna. I appreciate it."

* ✿ *

It was rare for Kennedy to see Mia, because she had taken on extra hours at work, and Kennedy always seemed to miss her on her days off. Knowing Mia's shift ended at four o'clock the following morning, Kennedy set her alarm for four-thirty.

"What are you doing awake?" asked Mia, as she walked through the door and found Kennedy on the couch reading a book.

"I wanted to surprise you." Kennedy threw her book on the coffee table and ran to grab a small stack of papers off the top of her desk. She handed them to Mia.

"What's this?" questioned Mia. She slowly began to read the forms, dropping down on the couch beside Kennedy. Comprehension dawned on Mia's face as she read the first few lines. "Really? Do you really think I can get a grant for school?"

"No doubt about it," Kennedy responded confidently. "All you need to do is fill out those forms and submit them with your last W-2 form and wait."

"I can't believe I might actually get to go to school," Mia breathed, excitement showing on her face.

"Quite frankly, I think it's about time," stated Kennedy. "So, how about you fill those out while I make us some breakfast? Then, I'll mail them on my way to work this morning, and, with any luck, you'll be enrolling in school next semester."

Kennedy jumped off the couch, pulling a still-stunned Mia up behind her. Heading toward the kitchen, Kennedy continued. "I've checked into the few Elementary Education programs around, and ASU has a pretty good one. You'll need to take a bunch of prerequisite classes, which—if I were you—I'd take from MCC. The classes are smaller there and probably a little easier. Then, once you fulfill the prerequisites, you can apply for the ASU program, and two years later you—Mia Middleton—can teach elementary school."

"I don't believe this!" Mia could hardly contain her excitement. "Thank you so much! I can't believe you would go to all that trouble for me."

Kennedy smiled quietly as she started making French toast. "It was no trouble at all," she said dismissively, and then shook the spatula at her friend. "Now, will you please start filling those out so you can eat and get to bed?"

❋ ✿ ❋

The next day, Kennedy's nervousness returned full force as she and Shauna pulled into the parking lot of the Chinese restaurant. For the entire car ride, Shauna had prattled on and on about how silk plants should rarely be used in the decoration of expensive homes. Kennedy listened patiently, all the while disagreeing wholeheartedly. Unless the owners had green thumbs or employed a gardener, they'd have dead or dying plants within a month. Wondering once again how Shauna came to work for one of the top design firms in Arizona, Kennedy glanced at her watch. Her only hope was that they would arrive first, forcing their no-name client to find them at their table.

Opening the door to the restaurant, Kennedy smoothed the polyester fabric of her new pale blue business suit and slung her black leather bag, containing a few design books, over her shoulder. She entered the dimly lit Chinese restaurant to find a waitress waiting to seat her.

"For two?" The waitress asked in a thick Chinese accent.

"We are meeting someone," explained Shauna quickly. "Is there a gentleman here who is expecting two others?"

It was then that Kennedy saw a familiar face sitting at one of the tables. Grinning, Braxton stood and walked over to them. "Hi!"

"Oh, Braxton!" Kennedy said, smiling. "What are you doing here?"

Looking slightly perplexed, yet still giving her a half smile, he answered slowly, "I'm meeting you here." Kennedy's widened eyes gave her away, and Braxton started laughing. "Kennedy, if you didn't know who I was on the phone, why didn't you just ask?"

Kennedy was still trying to make sense of everything as she defended herself, "You never gave me the chance." She was completely confused. Why would Braxton want to meet with her about decorating some new homes? Did he work for a developer or something? She desperately attempted to draw some sort of conclusion as Braxton turned to introduce himself to Kennedy's supervisor.

He stopped cold when he met Shauna's eyes. "Oh, so you're Kennedy's supervisor," he stated flatly.

Now Kennedy was nonplussed. The two already seemed to know each other, and it definitely didn't seem to be a friendly relationship.

"Yes, I am," Shauna replied with even less enthusiasm. "So, it appears as though you may want to hire us after all?" Her question held a bit of sarcasm.

Kennedy was both puzzled and uncomfortable. Deciding to interrupt the discussion before the room got any chillier, Kennedy made a suggestion. "Hey, how about we have a seat and get some food?"

Braxton hesitantly returned his attention back to Kennedy. Stepping aside, he gestured toward the table and followed behind them as they took their seats, wondering what he had gotten himself into.

They all ordered and waited for their food in an uncomfortable silence. Kennedy could stand it no longer and finally said, "So, Braxton, I'm a little confused. Do you work for some developer? What were you talking about when you said new homes? And why in the world would you call me instead of someone with more experience, like Shauna?" Kennedy wasn't quite sure what it was she said, but the tension somehow became worse. She was sick of it. "Okay, there is obviously some history between the two of you, and I have no idea what, but what do you say we lay our personal issues aside and talk business?"

Braxton gave a slight smile. "They aren't exactly personal issues, Kennedy," he explained. "In a nutshell, I own a developing company called Taylor Homes. Typically, we provide people with high quality, affordable housing; however, we have recently acquired a prime piece of land out in Gilbert where we are finishing up on the construction of five larger, more high-end homes. We have an in-house design crew, but they're only used to dealing with the smaller homes we construct; therefore, we wanted to contract with a more experienced design firm for this project. I called you, because I know you and trust you and thought it wouldn't hurt to get a proposal from you. I need five model homes decorated by the first of the year."

He paused for a moment, before continuing the explanation. "Shauna actually approached me several months ago, wanting us to replace our own design crew with your company. Besides being unwilling to do that to my employees, I thought Interior Essentials was far too expensive. I basically told her in no uncertain terms to take a hike."

"Really?" Kennedy had to stop herself from smiling. What she would have given to hear that particular conversation.

He took a quick look in Shauna's direction. "I'm afraid I did. And let me tell you, she wasn't too happy with my answer, so I suppose that's why you can say there is a 'history' between us." He refrained from saying out loud that he thought Shauna pompous and overbearing.

Through all this explanation, Shauna remained uncharacteristically quiet; however, Braxton and Kennedy practically forced her into speaking when both pairs of eyes stared at her expectantly.

She finally spoke. "Well, Mr. Taylor, I must say that it's a bit of surprise to see you approaching our company. I had thought you cut all ties with us. Evidently, Kennedy here has happily changed your mind." She sounded polite, but Kennedy and Braxton were not fooled. It was only a façade. "So, how about we let bygones be bygones and you tell us what you'd like us to do."

Braxton didn't like the thought of working with Shauna in the least. Figuring he'd take that issue up later without Kennedy around, he nodded and became businesslike. "I brought the floor plans with me." He pulled a stack of house plans from his briefcase, spreading them out on the table in front of Kennedy. "Well, at least three of the five anyhow. I couldn't find the other two, so I'll have to get those to you at another time."

Kennedy and Shauna looked over the floor plans carefully, setting them aside when the food arrived a moment later. After about five minutes more of uncomfortable silence, Shauna was the first to speak. "We will need all five plans before we can arrange a proposal or estimate for you." Her tone was final. It sounded as though their lunch meeting was over before they had even finished eating. She even put down her fork and took the napkin off her lap for emphasis.

Kennedy wasn't about to go, though. She was starving, and the food was unbelievably good. Shauna would just have to wait. Ignoring Shauna's cue, Kennedy asked Braxton, "So, just out of curiosity, if you do choose to contract with us, are you willing to give us free rein, or will we need to clear every decision with you?"

"I'll have to confer with the head of our own interior design department, but I can't see them wanting to get in your way too much." He sipped his egg drop soup. "By the way, do you happen to have any examples of your work with you?" He pointedly asked the question of Kennedy. Obviously feeling slighted and seeing that Kennedy wasn't about to leave before she finished her lunch, Shauna abruptly excused herself and went to the ladies room.

Kennedy pushed her plate aside and pulled out the two Interior Essentials books she had grabbed before leaving. "As you know, I haven't been with the company for long, so none of my work is in here, but this will give you a general idea about the kind of work Shauna and our firm produces. And this," she lugged out her own portfolio, "is the portfolio I put together in college, so you can see the kind of stuff I like."

Braxton ignored the Interior Essentials books and delved directly into Kennedy's own work, wanting to know what her tastes were like.

Kennedy watched him closely as he looked through it. "Do you like it?"

"Very much." He was relieved to find that he really did like what he saw.

Closing the portfolio, he returned it to Kennedy. He didn't even bother opening the company's books. "Listen, Kennedy, I really like your style. Is there any way I can work with you without your supervisor?"

"I'm afraid not."

He grimaced. "Well, all right then. I'll stop by your place tonight with the other two floor plans. You and Shauna make me an estimate, and we'll go from there."

"Deal." Grinning, she tore open her fortune cookie and read aloud, "Your career will soon take off in leaps and bounds." Kennedy laughed, unable to resist saying, "I really like this restaurant."

❋ Chapter 7 ❋

T HE NEXT TWO months flew by. Kennedy was asked to be the first counselor in her ward's Relief Society, so with her new responsibilities, combined with work, she barely found time to miss Chris anymore. It was only on rare occasions that she would take his picture out of her top chest drawer and allow herself to remember how perfect her life had once been. Just as her mom had predicted, though, she came to Arizona, got busy, and things got easier. When Kennedy did find the time to think and remember, the vivid pain was still there. The ache was still there. The yearning was still there. And the question still loomed: Would she ever see him again? Knowing these thoughts would gain her nothing but agitation, Kennedy busied herself as much as possible.

Braxton had brought by the floor plans as promised, and she had followed up a few days later by faxing him an estimate. She knew their prices were high, but there was nothing she could do about that yet. Interior Essentials had a standard estimate system. The only way Kennedy could help lower the costs was to cut the costs of the actual supplies they would need to decorate. Kennedy explained the situation to Braxton, and he said he would think about it and get back to her. Apparently he'd decided to hire them, because less than two days later he'd contacted Shauna.

Later that afternoon, Shauna called Kennedy into her office. Not one to beat around the bush, Shauna began brusquely. "Taylor Homes has contracted Interior Essentials to decorate the five model homes." Shauna glared, not bothering to mask her anger. Kennedy could practically see the hatred in Shauna's eyes. "Being as busy as

I am, I have decided to turn the project over to you, and since you obviously won't be able to do it alone, I have arranged for Suzi and Katie to help you." She dismissed Kennedy with a wave of her hand. "We'll see just how successful you will be in the real world," she said cruelly.

Walking out of Shauna's office, Kennedy was stunned. What had Braxton said to Shauna? Had he really arranged for Kennedy to head up the design team? Kennedy never thought that Braxton could have completely bypassed Shauna. And Suzi and Katie? The two girls were nice, but they had even less experience than Kennedy. She realized Shauna had, in all likelihood, arranged it on purpose, hoping Kennedy would fail. This possibility only strengthened her resolve to do the best job she—or anyone else—could do, but she still felt uncomfortable with the way things had played out.

Despite her worries, Kennedy couldn't help but feel excited. For the first few months, Kennedy had worked more as a secretary for Shauna than as a design assistant. Her knowledge of interior design was definitely not increasing, and that frustrated her. If it weren't for Braxton, she would probably have remained the glorified secretary indefinitely. Kennedy decided to shrug off Shauna's comments and went to track down Suzi and Katie.

Suzi and Katie were newcomers like herself, but they were equally determined to do the job well, and Kennedy was grateful for their enthusiasm. The three of them began pulling late hours, working furiously to complete all of the preliminary designs before the houses were ready for them to decorate. They had met with the head designer from Taylor Homes and, just as Braxton had predicted, they were given carte blanche on the project.

Time flew by, and soon it was the week of Thanksgiving. She had originally planned to drive home for the long weekend to visit her family, but she realized that in order to beat the deadline and finish the models before Christmas, she would have to work the entire holiday weekend. With a heavy heart, she phoned her mom.

"I'm so sorry, Mom. I really wanted to come home this weekend."

"Boy, this Braxton fellow must be a complete slave driver."

Kennedy smiled at the absurd mental image of Braxton forcing her to work. "No, Mom, it's not that at all. In fact, if he knew I was going to stay here instead of go home for Thanksgiving, he'd probably drive me out of the state."

"Well, for heaven's sake, let him know then!" her mother teased.

"No, Mom. I'm determined to have these homes decorated before Christmas. We are getting so close. The first of the five homes has already been painted and the furniture arranged, so this weekend we need to hang up curtains, make up the beds, and put up all the finishing touches. The painting is in progress in two of the other homes, and once I get Braxton's final approval for a few last-minute changes, we'll be ready to start the last two homes as well. If everything goes smoothly, we'll finish them just in time."

Olivia smiled at her daughter's enthusiasm. "Well, all right, sweetie. We'll miss you this weekend, but we'll keep our fingers crossed that you'll still be coming home for Christmas."

"Oh, I'll definitely be home for Christmas," Kennedy replied. "There is no way I would ever miss out on our annual Scrabble tournament."

Olivia laughed at her daughter. "Well, I should probably warn you, then, that your father and I have been reading the dictionary every night before we go to sleep."

"And that's supposed to worry me?" Kennedy said. "Everyone knows how difficult it is for you and Dad to stay awake at night to read. With your current study habits, not to mention your short-term memory problems, I'd be surprised if you've added one new word to your current vocabulary."

"Well, we'll have to see about that, won't we?"

Kennedy grinned. "You're funny, Mom, but I better get going. I want to get Braxton's approval tonight on these paint and flooring samples."

"I thought they already gave you the go-ahead on everything."

"I know, but Braxton really has good taste, and with Shauna scrutinizing my every move, I need the assurance from Braxton that the job we're doing for him will make Interior Essentials look good. He probably thinks I'm annoying and incapable of making decisions, but I need to feel secure in what we're doing before it's too late to make any changes."

"I see. Well, have a good night, then. And promise me that you'll eat some turkey and homemade rolls for Thanksgiving."

"You have my word."

Kennedy smiled as she hung up the phone. She was sad to think about missing Thanksgiving at home but was really looking forward to viewing the finished project. Thank goodness she enjoyed her work so much.

✳ ✴ ✳

Braxton arrived home late that evening after an incredibly long day at the office. Noticing the message light blinking on his phone, he quickly punched the button and opened the refrigerator to examine its sorry contents.

"Hello, Mr. Taylor. This is Miss America, and I was calling to inform you that your name has been drawn for a free date with *moi*! Please call me back as soon as possible in order to confirm. I am an incredibly busy and wanted woman, you know." The familiar voice then left a phone number and hung up.

Chuckling, Braxton found that his long day was suddenly looking brighter, even though it was already nine o'clock. Forgetting all about his hunger, he grabbed the phone and dialed Kennedy's number.

"Hello?"

"Hi. I was looking for Miss America," Braxton stated. "I was told that I have won a date with her."

"Oh . . . yes," Kennedy replied slowly, as if preparing Braxton for bad news. "Then I am sorry to say that you didn't call soon enough. Her schedule is now booked for the next ten years. By that time, she probably won't be as beautiful or famous, so you may not want to wait."

"That's too bad," Braxton murmured. "Perhaps you'd like to go with me instead?"

"Oh, sure, that won't be a problem."

"Great. When are you free?"

"What about tonight?"

"You sure don't waste any time, do you?"

"Nope. My schedule is completely open. I'm not nearly as talented or beautiful. When can I come over?"

"I beg to differ on the talented and beautiful remark, and you can come over whenever." Braxton was highly amused by the direction the conversation was taking.

"Great! Just tell me how to get there, and I'll be right over."

Braxton suddenly found himself wondering if she was being serious. "Are you kidding?"

"No." Kennedy sounded happy to have fooled him. "I have some samples I want to get your okay on."

"Kennedy, we've already given you the go-ahead for whatever you think is best."

"I know, but I'd feel much better with your approval. It was your interference, after all, that made Shauna despise me even more than she already did."

He sighed. "I'll just come over to your place then."

"You always have to come by here, and I refuse to ask that of you when it is my insecurities that need your reassurance. Besides, I have to run by and pick a sample up from a coworker who happens to also live in south Tempe, so if you will kindly give me directions to your house, I will be over in a jiffy."

For some reason, Braxton wasn't comfortable with the idea of Kennedy seeing his home. Trying to think of a way out, he grasped at the first thought that came to his mind. "Well, just tell me where she is, and I'll pick up what you need and then come over."

Kennedy laughed out loud. "Don't be silly, Brax. Just give me directions. Besides, Stacey has gushed about your beautiful home one too many times, so you have to know I've been dying to see it."

Seeing no way out, he finally gave her directions. He placed the phone back on the receiver, still wondering why he didn't want Kennedy to come over. Most people thought his home was too extravagant and that he was flaunting his money. He didn't see it that way, but he still worried about what Kennedy would think.

Resigning himself to the fact that she would be arriving within the hour and that there was nothing he could do about it, he started straightening up. He threw an empty pizza box into the trash can and quickly wiped off the counter. After washing the few dishes that had been piling up in the sink, he grabbed his basketball shoes from off the family room floor, walked down the hall, and threw them into his bedroom. Clothes and magazines lay in disarray all over the cluttered room. He grimaced and quickly shut the door, making a mental note not to show Kennedy the master suite, should she ask to see the house.

He was just wrapping up the vacuum cord when the doorbell rang. Shoving the vacuum into a nearby closet, he ran to the foyer and opened the door, feeling slightly out of breath.

"Wow, Brax, you neglected to tell me you lived in a mansion," Kennedy said, ducking under his arm as she let herself in. "I might have known, though, judging by that bed you let me borrow."

"That bed was donated to me by some store that was, no doubt, hoping for some free advertising if we used it in one of our models." He shrugged and closed the door, turning toward Kennedy. "It didn't really fit with any of the decor in the homes we were building at the time, so I decided to bring it here."

"I see," Kennedy said as she glanced up and around in awe. "You don't mind if I have a look around before we get to work, do you?" Pulling open the door off to the right of the foyer, she strolled inside what was obviously his study.

"I don't think I have a choice, do I?"

"Nope, not really," Kennedy teased, looking at the beautiful built-in mahogany bookcases and cupboards that lined three of the four walls. Braxton obviously liked to read, because the book-cases contained hundreds of books, covering every topic from home building to John Grisham's latest novel. A matching mahogany desk, cluttered with a laptop and papers, and a large leather chair were the only other furniture in the room.

Kennedy reverently ran her fingers along the edge of the desk, feeling the beautifully carved wood. Smiling, she glanced up at Braxton. "Let me guess. An office supply store had an extra desk they hoped you could take off their hands."

"Not so lucky. The desk was actually my father's. He purchased it when we sold off our first home. He said we'd be needing some fancy furniture to do business with our high-profile clients." His expression clouded slightly. "After I built the house, I had the desk moved here from the office."

Kennedy knew from her brief conversation with Becca at the

stake social that Braxton's father had passed away, but she didn't know any of the details. She didn't want to sound nosy, but she couldn't stifle her curiosity. "What happened to your father?" she asked quietly. Realizing she was prying, she rapidly apologized. "I'm sorry. I shouldn't have asked."

Glancing up quickly, he forced a smile. "No, that's okay." For some reason, he didn't mind talking to Kennedy. "He died in a car crash a few years ago. I won't bother you with all the details, but a woman ran into him. She had two of her own children in the car, and her oldest didn't make it either."

Kennedy's expression mirrored his pain. She couldn't imagine losing one of her parents or an innocent little child. Placing her hand on his arm, she said the only thing she could think of. "I am so sorry."

He found comfort in her touch. "It was a long time ago," he stated simply.

"Yeah, but I don't believe that time heals all wounds—at least not completely."

Braxton smiled at her understanding. "Me neither."

"Did you ever talk to that woman?"

"Yeah." Braxton took a deep breath. "I called her a few months afterward. I don't even remember what we talked about, but it made me feel much better."

Kennedy cocked her head at him, admiration evident on her face. "That must have taken a lot of courage."

He gazed at her in return, feeling slightly embarrassed and yet oddly more at peace than he had in a long time.

Removing her hand, she quickly linked her arm through his, and changed the subject. "Now, are you going to show me around, or is this a self-guided tour?"

Braxton acquiesced. He led Kennedy out of the study and into the family room and kitchen area, wondering why he had been concerned with having her over. He showed her the living room with the vaulted ceiling and white baby grand piano. He showed her the spacious spare bedrooms—including the one with the beautiful hand-carved bed she had borrowed. He showed her the large game room and home theater, the backyard, the swimming pool, the tennis court, and even the garage—at her insistence. He distracted her with a beautiful Monet print on the wall as he sped her past the double doors that led into his bedroom. His tour finally came to a close, and he thought he had fooled her, but she obviously didn't miss much.

"Wait. I haven't seen the master suite yet. Where's that?"

"Sorry, I'm afraid my room is, uh . . ." he paused, as if searching for the correct phrase to use. "Under construction," he finished lamely.

"Ah, I see." She nodded, backing away from him slowly. Suddenly she grinned wickedly, spun on her heel and darted down the hall. "Be right back!" she called over her shoulder.

Before he realized what she was doing, she had a fairly significant lead. "Darn her!" he grumbled, running after her down the hall. He only hoped that she didn't know which doors led into his bedroom. Unluckily, the double doors were a dead giveaway, and he arrived just after she had pulled them open.

"Braxton Taylor." She shook her head, placing her hands on her hips and using her best disappointed-mother tone. "I'm shocked!" She surveyed the disaster in his bedroom. "Am I to understand that you didn't have room for a closet in this massive home?" She was trying hard not to laugh.

Grabbing Kennedy by the arm, Braxton began pulling her toward the doors. "Kennedy, I told you this room was off-limits. You can see it some other time."

Resisting with all her might, Kennedy tried to reason with him. "But I've already seen what a slob you are, Brax, so you might as well let me see the rest of it." Unfortunately, she could control her giggles no longer, which served to strengthen Braxton's resolve to remove her from the room as quickly as possible. He finally pushed her into the hall, closing the doors firmly behind him.

"Oh, come on," she taunted. "We could play Mary Poppins and pick up your room."

"No." His voice was firm, and his grip on her arm tightened as he led her down the hall.

"But—"

"No." He pulled her into the family room and placed her in his recliner. He was trying so hard to be stern, but Kennedy could see a spark of humor in his eyes. "Now, where are the samples you wanted me to see?"

"On the kitchen counter," she replied obediently, folding her arms like a penitent child. "And I do apologize. Had I known the state of your room, I would never have included it in my tour."

Finally, he let out a chuckle as he went to retrieve the fabric samples. "Right."

Kennedy smiled at Braxton as he threw the samples on the floor next to the recliner and casually laid down beside them, with his arm propping up his head. "But at least now I know you're human," she said.

"What's that supposed to mean?"

"Well, I can stop being intimidated by you, now that I know you aren't perfect."

"Yeah, like you have ever been intimidated by me."

Ignoring his remark, Kennedy continued, "And wait until Stacey gets a load of this. Won't she be surprised!" She plopped down on the floor in front of him and started sorting through the samples, not noticing the confused look on Braxton's face. "Now, on to business." She then proceeded to show Braxton the various paint and fabric samples she had in mind for the last two model homes. They slowly went through the pile, with Kennedy thoroughly explaining all of her ideas. It took a little longer than she thought, but with Braxton's help, she happily made all the final decisions.

As Braxton was mulling over the last of the fabric swatches she had brought, Kennedy looked around at the spacious family room once again, taking note that his house was grand, but that it had few furnishings or decorations. In a way, it felt empty. She also realized that aside from the few pictures she saw of his father in the study, she hadn't seen any other pictures of people in the house.

Interrupting the silence, she questioned without thinking. "Hey, Brax, other than your father, why don't you have any pictures of your family up?" She studied him curiously.

He had to give Kennedy some credit. She definitely didn't miss much, and she wasn't afraid to speak her mind. Clearing his throat, he thought how to answer the uncomfortable question. Figuring he might as well be candid, he explained, "When my father and I joined the Church, my mother was furious. She immediately filed for divorce and left with my two younger sisters. We tried to contact them a few times, but they wanted nothing to do with us. My father never gave up, so, after he died, I tried to call my mom to give her the news. She hung up as soon as she found out who it was. I've pretty much given up having any sort of relationship with them."

Kennedy looked at Braxton with concern. "Wow, you've had it pretty tough, haven't you?"

He gave a bitter laugh. "You know, we're told that God will never give us trials that are more than we can bear, but He sure knows how to stretch our limits."

Kennedy nodded thoughtfully. "You know, in a morbid way, it's kind of flattering."

He looked over at her inquiringly.

"Well," she explained, "Heavenly Father obviously knows that you're a strong person." He still looked a little perplexed, so she tried to clarify. "My parents used to tell me that God always gives the greatest trials to the people that are the strongest because He knows they can handle them—that the trials will serve to strengthen their character and make them that much better. Therefore, you can surmise that people who are dealt difficult hands in this life and come out on top are truly remarkable." Smiling, she continued. "And knowing what little I know about you, I'd say that's definitely true in your case."

"Thanks, Kennedy, I appreciate that." He was finding that not only was Kennedy full of wit and charm, but she was full of understanding and compassion as well. In only a few hours, she had made him feel much better about himself and his situation. He realized, for the first time since his father died, that he felt truly happy and content. He knew that a large part of that was due to the woman sitting on the floor next to him. He was definitely becoming more enamored every day.

"Ah, don't mention it." Kennedy smiled as she stretched her arms over her head and yawned. "Boy, I'm tired. It's probably getting pretty late." Standing, she craned her neck to get a view of the clock on the oven in the kitchen. She about died when she saw the time.

"Holy cow! It's nearly one o'clock in the morning! I am so sorry I've been here so long." She rushed to gather up the fabric swatches.

"You know, I never thought time could pass this quickly looking at material," Braxton commented dryly. "Perhaps I should start frequenting fabric stores."

"Just be careful of the crowds you find in those places," Kennedy said. "I hear they can get out of hand sometimes."

Chuckling, Braxton helped carry the box of swatches out to her car. Then he opened the driver's side door for her to get in. "Hey, thanks for coming over tonight. Believe it or not, I had fun—even though I'm still upset with you for barging into my bedroom."

Ignoring his bait, Kennedy simply smiled. "I had fun too, and I really appreciate your input." Ducking into her car, she called, "I guess I'll see you later," and waved as she pulled out of his driveway.

❋ Chapter 8 ❋

M IA AND KENNEDY were both invited to spend Thanksgiving with
Becca, while Stacey invited Braxton for dinner with her family.
It was fun to finally meet all of Becca's family, but Kennedy felt
the need to duck out as soon as she felt it wouldn't be impolite. She
had work to do, and she needed to get started. Besides, she had fulfilled her promise to her mother—she'd eaten a good Thanksgiving
dinner.

Kennedy worked hard all weekend long at decorating the first
house that had already been painted, carpeted, and tiled. She met
Suzi and Katie on Friday morning. The three of them worked late
into the night hanging curtains, making beds, papering walls, and
hanging shelves, pictures, and other decorative paraphernalia. By
late Saturday night, they were putting the final touches on the first
home. One home down, four to go.

❋ ❋ ❋

Hanging her keys on the hook by the door and closing the door
behind her, Kennedy glanced around gloomily, noting that there
wasn't a Christmas decoration to be found anywhere in her apartment. Here it was, eight days after Thanksgiving, and it didn't even
look like Christmas. What a pathetic excuse for an interior designer
she was.

Because they were ahead of schedule, Kennedy had demanded
that Katie and Suzi take the night off, and the three of them agreed
to meet Saturday morning to finish up the second, and largest, of
the houses.

"B. J. just called for you," drawled a voice. Kennedy hadn't noticed Stacey sprawled on the floor, reading from a chemistry book.

"Hi, Stace!" Kennedy replied. "Where's Becca?"

"She had a date with Jason, remember?" Stacey stated emotionlessly.

"Oh, that's right." Ever since the opening social, Becca had made a point of going with Kennedy to all the ward activities, even dragging Stacey along sometimes. Becca and Jason had made a fast connection and had begun to spend more and more time together. It was a pleasant surprise when Becca began going to church with Kennedy most Sundays. In the meantime, Stacey had finished her discussions and went to church with Braxton every time he asked her, but she was always ready with an excuse whenever Becca and Kennedy asked if she'd like to go with them. She continually told Braxton she just needed more time. Not wanting to push her, he backed off but still stopped by their apartment quite frequently.

Kennedy worked late much of the time and wasn't home for the majority of his visits, but she always heard about them from an excited Becca, who seemed certain that Braxton was falling head over heels in love with her best friend. Stacey, on the other hand, appeared less enthusiastic, which seemed strange to Kennedy. After all, if Kennedy had a handsome, witty, kind, and fun-loving guy coming to visit her all the time, she would be thrilled—if that guy's name were Chris. But she refused to dwell on it, especially when her favorite holiday was quickly approaching.

Realizing that Stacey was looking at her expectantly, Kennedy raised her eyebrows in question. "What?"

"I said that B. J. called for you." Her voice remained lifeless.

"Yeah, I heard you. I'll call him back in a sec. I'm sure it has something to do with work, and right now, I'm starving and don't want to think about work." Kennedy wandered into the kitchen, opened the fridge, and realized immediately that she needed to go grocery shopping.

"He likes you," Stacey said abruptly.

Kennedy was confused. "Who? What are you talking about?" She closed the refrigerator door in frustration, wondering what she could concoct to feed her grumbling stomach.

"B. J.," Stacey stated almost coldly. "He likes you."

All thoughts of hunger ceased as Stacey's ludicrous words indexed themselves in her mind. Wide-eyed, Kennedy appeared around the corner of the kitchen and stared down at Stacey. "Don't be crazy, Stacey. He only called to talk about work—I guarantee it."

"I realize that," Stacey said heatedly. She closed her chemistry book and sat up. "But I'm not just talking about tonight. He always stops by to see you, and he's always calling you."

Kennedy couldn't help rolling her eyes. It had already been such a long day. Why was Stacey acting like this? "First of all, Stacey, he calls me about work and only work." She placed a great deal of emphasis on the word *work*. "And second, he comes by to see *you*, not me. I mean, good grief, I'm not even here most of the time when he does come over!"

"Yeah, and I find it interesting that he stays much longer when you are here."

"What?" Kennedy was feeling the beginnings of irritation, and Stacey was sounding more and more absurd. Kennedy wondered why they were even having this conversation.

Stacey looked down at the floor, and Kennedy could see her blinking rapidly as she tried to keep the tears from her eyes. Finding some of her annoyance melting away at the site of a genuinely anguished roommate, Kennedy carefully crouched down beside Stacey and asked softly, "Stace, are you okay? What's going on?"

"I'm so sorry, Kennedy," Stacey sniffled. "I'm so jealous of the time you two spend together on work stuff. It's just that I like him so much, and I don't think that he cares about me at all like that."

"Of course he does," Kennedy comforted softly. "How could he not? You are intelligent, sweet, and fun—not to mention gorgeous. He'd be crazy not to fall for you."

"Do you really think so?" Stacey looked hopeful.

"Of course I do." Kennedy grinned, attempting to lighten the tone. "I've heard Becca's rendition of his visits, and from what she says, he definitely likes you as more than just a friend."

"Becca exaggerates. We never go on any real dates."

"You know what, Stace?" Kennedy confided. "To be honest, I don't think Braxton has gone on a date with anyone in a long time."

Kennedy winked. "But the fact that he stops by so often to see you speaks volumes."

Stacey threw her arms around Kennedy. "Thanks. I am so sorry for what I said earlier."

"Oh, forget it." Kennedy waved off the apology. "Now, I'm starving and have no food. How would you like to go out for dinner somewhere?"

"Sure!" Stacey replied and then smiled. "Maybe you could call B. J. back and invite him along."

"If you're sure you want me to."

"I'm sure." Stacey jumped up from the floor. "I'll go get ready."

Kennedy laughed at her roommate and picked up the phone, pressing the speed dial button with Braxton's number. "Hello?" He answered after the third ring.

"Hi Brax, it's Kennedy."

They talked about work for a little while, and as they were wrapping things up, Braxton asked, "What are you doing tonight?"

"I'm famished, so Stacey and I are going to grab some dinner. Want to come?" she asked casually.

"Sure, I'll just stick this pot pie back in the freezer and be right over."

"Great! We'll see you soon."

During dinner, Kennedy told Braxton and Stacey of her plans to buy Christmas decorations for their apartment. They were pleased with the idea and agreed to go along with Kennedy to help pick out a tree and some decorations. Braxton even asked the two girls to help him decorate his own house. Of course, it didn't take much convincing for them to agree—Kennedy, because she loved to decorate, and Stacey, because she loved Braxton.

"But isn't it too soon to get a tree?" Braxton asked as he listened to Kennedy talk about how she was going to decorate the tree in their apartment.

"Not for an artificial tree."

"You can't get an artificial tree," Braxton accused.

"Why not?"

"Because you just can't."

"Oh, there's an argument for you," Kennedy said smartly. "Ever thought of leaving the development business and becoming an attorney?"

Rolling his eyes, Braxton ignored her comment and continued, "It just wouldn't be Christmas without a genuine, pine-smelling, needle-falling Christmas tree."

"Well, it's not Christmas without snow either," Kennedy pointed out, "but that doesn't seem to stop you Southerners from celebrating the holiday."

"Yes, but snow is out of our control. Christmas trees are not." Braxton thought he had effectively ended the discussion.

"Not so." Kennedy's eyes twinkled. "Ever heard of snow machines?"

Shaking his head, Braxton looked to Stacey for help.

Grinning, Stacey merely shrugged her shoulders. "I plead the fifth," she said, taking a small bite of her salad.

"Well, Brax, you are more than welcome to wait two more weeks for your fire-hazard of a Christmas tree, but not me," Kennedy stated with assurance. "I prefer the perfectly shaped, low-maintenance tree that you can have on display from now until New Year's."

"Fine, have it your way." Braxton's tone held a note of triumph. "But rest assured that the model homes we have open will only feature real, genuine, pine-smelling Christmas trees."

Kennedy responded by sticking her tongue out at Braxton.

Once dinner was over, the three of them ventured off to the store, ready to get some shopping done. Knowing that Stacey probably wanted some time alone with Braxton, Kennedy insisted that she shop for the perfect tree and ornaments, while they look for lights, garland, and of course, hot chocolate mix.

The three of them met up at the checkout counter, purchased their items, loaded them into the back of Braxton's truck, and sped back to the apartment. Once they transported everything up the stairs, Kennedy disappeared into her room, reappearing moments later with speakers and her iPod, which was loaded with her favorite Christmas music. The three of them spent the evening decorating and singing along to "Santa Claus is Coming to Town." Becca and Jason returned just in time to help them put the final touches on the tree. They all cheered when Kennedy plugged in the lights, and the tree became aglow with hundreds of tiny white lights.

After turning off all the living room lights so the tree glowed even more brilliantly, Kennedy decided it was definitely time for hot chocolate—even if it was Arizona. Braxton sauntered in just as she was finishing up. "So, I suppose that my house will have to wait until tomorrow."

"Will you be okay to go one more night?" Kennedy asked with mock concern.

Braxton chuckled. "I'm not sure how I'm ever going to get any sleep, though—with all the anticipation."

"Oh, I'm sure you'll find a way." Kennedy said. "Besides, maybe we can convince Jason and Becca to come and lend a hand as well. And I think Mia's off tomorrow. We could all help. It'll be fun!"

"Aren't you sick of decorating yet?"

"I'll be ready for a break in a few weeks," she admitted. "But this is different. Who, in their right mind, would ever turn down an opportunity to decorate a gorgeously massive home for Christmas?"

Braxton smiled at her enthusiasm. "You really love Christmas, don't you?"

She filled several mugs with steaming hot chocolate. "It's the most magical time of the year. How could anyone not love it?" she asked. Kennedy passed two mugs to Braxton to help distribute.

✳ ✿ ✳

The following evening, Braxton opened his front door to a crowd of people. Some of the faces looked familiar, but most did not. Without a second thought, he deduced that Kennedy was behind whatever sort of evening this was going to turn out to be. Stepping aside, he opened the door wider and shrugged his shoulders, pasting a smile on his face as he gestured for them all to come in.

A few of the familiar faces grinned as they entered. "Hey there, Braxton! Thanks for having us over!"

As the people passed by, Braxton was able to get a glimpse of his driveway. Among the throng of vehicles scattered across it and the street, he saw Kennedy's car and Kennedy loading Stacey, Jason, Becca, and Mia up with a bunch of bags and boxes she was pulling from her trunk. It reminded him of a commercial he once saw in which thirty clowns exited one tiny VW Bug.

Shaking his head, Braxton strode into the driveway. "Kennedy Jackson!" he called.

Kennedy's head popped out of the trunk, her face all innocence. "You bellowed?"

Obviously not wanting to be around for any sort of lecture, Jason, Becca, Stacey, and Mia scurried past Braxton and into his house.

Folding his arms and widening his stance, Braxton simply stood there, staring at Kennedy with raised eyebrows, waiting for her to explain exactly why she had deemed it necessary to invite her entire ward over to his place.

Completely ignoring his implied question, Kennedy simply stated, "I'm glad you came out. I could use another hand to carry the rest of these bags inside."

"And what, pray tell, are in those bags?" Braxton asked without budging an inch.

"A few more Christmas decorations and groceries, of course." She grinned and placed a bag in Braxton's arms, followed immediately by another. Then she hefted a large box, balancing it on her hip, as she slammed the trunk closed.

"A few? My house is going to look like *Who*-ville from *How The Grinch Stole Christmas!*"

"Nonsense," she replied as she headed for the house. "It will be much more festive."

Braxton followed hot on her heels. "First of all, Kennedy, I already bought Christmas decorations yesterday with you, remember? Second, and more important, I never invited all these people over to my house."

"I know." She was being an imp, and he could tell that she knew it. "However, your house, as you know, is fairly large, and the stuff you bought yesterday won't go very far—believe me. As for the people, well, I invited them. I figured it would be a good time for you to get to know some new faces." She leaned in and whispered secretively, "I hear you aren't too social."

They had reached the front door, and Braxton caught her hand just as she was about to tug on the handle. "Listen, Kennedy. I'm not social because I have no desire to be. I go to church, and I fulfill my calling. That's all that's important to me, okay?"

"No, it's not okay," Kennedy explained calmly. "Braxton, those people in your house are incredible. They are friendly and a whole lot of fun. Regardless of whether you want them or not, you need friends."

"I have friends."

Raising her eyebrows in obvious disbelief, she replied, "The more the merrier."

"Not for everyone."

"Okay, fine." Kennedy was quickly losing her cool. "I'll go and un-invite all of them if that is what you'd like."

Knowing she was blowing smoke, Braxton nodded. "Good! I'd like that."

"You can't be serious!" She stamped her foot for emphasis as she glared at him.

Seeing the fuming look on Kennedy's face provided Braxton with a little retribution. "All right, they can stay." Braxton allowed a small smile to touch his lips. "But you owe me for this."

"Name your price."

"Dinner."

"Sure," Kennedy replied quickly. "You pick the restaurant."

"Oh, no." Braxton grinned, opening the door for her. "I want a home-cooked meal." He quickly pushed her into the throng of people before she had a chance to refute.

Braxton was immediately pulled into a game of charades, while Kennedy and Stacey set to work organizing Christmas decorations. Before long, everyone abandoned the game and went to help decorate. All the guys headed outside to hang the brightly colored outdoor lights Kennedy had purchased, while the girls wove greenery over the mantel on the fireplace, which Kennedy accented with red Christmas bells tied with gold ribbon. Kennedy had also purchased a dark blue denim stocking lined with fur for Braxton. They strung greenery over the banister above the basement stairs and along every shelf they could find. They strung it above the cabinets in the kitchen and around the outside of the front door. And, finally, Kennedy had brought over her prized Christmas decoration—a hand-carved wooden nativity from Jerusalem. Her sister Jackie had studied for a semester abroad in Jerusalem and brought it back for her, knowing how much Kennedy loved Christmas. Kennedy really had no room for it in her apartment and figured Braxton could use all the decorations he could get. Besides, it looked perfect nestled among the greenery on the mantle.

Braxton re-entered his home to find it completely transformed into Christmas. It was tasteful and festive, and he actually liked it! He scanned the room for Kennedy, finding her alone in the kitchen area where she was preparing snacks and drinks for everyone. As she filled a pitcher up with ice from the freezer, he came up behind her and whispered in her ear. "I suppose nobody will be calling me a grinch this year."

Jumping, Kennedy spun around to face him, almost bumping into him. She found his piercing blue eyes probing hers as his lips formed a slow, lazy smile. Her heart started pounding as she found herself forgetting to breathe. She suddenly realized she was staring at his mouth and took a step back. She tried to hide her embarrassment with a laugh. "You startled me." Struggling to regain her wits, Kennedy tried to recall what he'd said before. "Uh, don't worry. People won't be calling you a citizen of *Who*-ville either."

His smile broadened at her obvious loss of composure. "I know. And thank you. The house looks fantastic. I should have known I could trust you not to go overboard."

"I'm saving the overboard for your model homes," she replied pertly, and she quickly put more distance between them as she rounded the island to rearrange the food. Thankfully, someone called him away, and Kennedy was left alone with her disturbing thoughts for a moment. Luckily, no one had seemed to notice their uncomfortable tête-à-tête, but it made her feel deeply unsettled.

The rest of the evening flew by, and before Kennedy realized it, her watch read midnight. Reminding everyone that they had nine o'clock church in the morning, Kennedy was able to clear the premises, leaving only Stacey, Mia, Becca, Jason, and Kennedy to clean up. With all of them working, they straightened up the house in no time.

Kennedy carried the last empty box out to the garage and re-entered in time to hear Becca exclaim, "Hey, you two are under the mistletoe!"

Kennedy glanced up to find everyone staring at Stacey and Braxton, who, sure enough, stood directly under the mistletoe hanging from the ceiling fan in the family room.

He smiled down at Stacey. "We sure are," he drawled. He picked up a giggling Stacey, spun her around, and planted a quick kiss on her forehead.

The sudden stab of jealousy Kennedy felt surprised her. She had to force her lips to smile in time to cover her reaction. Reminding herself that she was not in the running for Braxton's affections, she busily shoved the last of the chip dip into his fridge and quickly made her excuses to go. Mia came with her, but Stacey stayed to catch a ride with Jason and Becca.

As they left, Mia was exuberant. "That was so much fun! Thanks for inviting me."

"Mia, you are always invited. I'm just glad you were able to get the night off."

"Yeah, me too," Mia said, laughing excitedly. "And in only one month, I'll be able to quit altogether and get on my way to becoming a kindergarten teacher."

"And a very good one at that," Kennedy spoke warmly.

"I owe it all to you," Mia said sincerely.

"So, how's Jerry?" Kennedy effectively steered the conversation away from herself.

Mia looked a little depressed. "I think I've finally come to grips with the fact that he'll never be interested in me."

"Well, he's not the brightest bulb then, is he?" Kennedy rolled down the window to feel the cool night breeze.

"You're so sweet, Kenn."

"Brad's much more intelligent, you know," Kennedy hinted.

"What do you mean?"

"I mean," Kennedy explained pointedly, "that he is on his way to being halfway in love with you."

"Brad?" Mia rolled her eyes. "I don't think so. And besides, I don't like him like that."

"Too bad," Kennedy murmured, "because he's sure a great guy." Then, throwing a playful smile at Mia, she added, "He'd sure make one heck of a husband for any kindergarten teacher."

Mia giggled, but remained uncharacteristically quiet for the remainder of the drive home, which allowed Kennedy's thoughts to wander in a most troubling direction—Braxton. She realized now that she was starting to fall for him, and the thought brought a sickening twinge to her stomach. Why? Why him? *Good grief, you are such an idiot*, she silently berated herself. Stacey had already staked her claim on him, and Kennedy had no right to vie for his attentions as well. She would just have to bury her feelings and try to distance herself, which would be difficult to do while she was still working with him. Once she was finished, though, she could steal away to her family's home for Christmas and attempt to put him from her mind.

Later that night, while Kennedy was lying in bed, attempting to go to sleep, she realized with a start that she hadn't thought of Chris in a very long time.

✳ ❋ ✳

Walking around the outside of his home toward his garage, intending to unplug the outdoor Christmas lights, Braxton was startled when they suddenly flicked off of their own accord. Wondering if a fuse had blown in one of the strands, he rounded the corner and came to the outlet. He had to laugh when he saw the timer Kennedy must have added after they had finished. That girl forgot nothing. She was amazing.

He had to admit that he'd had a great time with everyone there. As Kennedy promised, the people she invited were fun, friendly, and terrific company, and it was all thanks to Kennedy. The more he learned about her, the more he found himself thinking of her, and he did that almost constantly these days.

Going back inside, Braxton wandered through all the rooms, flipping off any lights that were on. Reaching to flip the switch in the family room, he glanced above the mantle on the fireplace, noticing for the first time the sole stocking hanging there. He walked over to investigate it. It was then that he saw the beautiful hand-carved nativity. He remembered Kennedy mentioning it when they were decorating her apartment, saying she wished they had a fireplace with a mantle so she could display her favorite Christmas adornment. They had tried to find a fitting place for it but gave up after they realized that there really was nowhere. And now, here it was, nestled skillfully amongst the greenery on the mantle. He was touched that Kennedy would freely loan him something so special to her. Carefully, he ran his fingers over the smooth carved wood, amazed at the skill of the carver. For the first time, his house felt like a home, rather than a casual residence, and he reveled in the warmth.

Finally, he flicked off the last of the lights and headed for his bedroom, making a mental note to phone Kennedy the following day and thank her once again—in addition to reminding her about the dinner she still owed him.

✿ Chapter 9 ✿

Kennedy, I need you to get me some coffee." Shauna's irritating voice interrupted the to-do list Kennedy was in the middle of writing.

Kennedy sighed and put down her pen. "Be right there." The infrequent days that Kennedy actually spent in the office were becoming more and more frustrating. It seemed as if Shauna was devising ways to disrupt Kennedy's work by sending her on nonsensical errands.

After pouring a cup of coffee, Kennedy entered Shauna's office and placed the mug on the desk. "Will there be anything else?" she asked.

Before Shauna could answer, the front receptionist entered, carrying a large bouquet of roses wrapped in cellophane. "These are for you," the receptionist told Shauna excitedly, setting the arrangement next to the mug of coffee.

"How beautiful!" Kennedy exclaimed, bending over to smell the flowers. "Someone's obviously thinking about you."

Before Kennedy knew what was happening, Shauna grabbed the bouquet and tossed it into her garbage can. "That will be all," she snapped.

Kennedy looked at the receptionist with raised eyebrows as the two left the office together.

"I would have taken the roses," the receptionist whispered before heading back to her desk. "My boyfriend could use a little friendly competition."

Chuckling, Kennedy returned to her to-do list, wondering about the story behind the flowers. Realizing she knew nothing about Shauna's personal life, Kennedy's mind began to wander. Was she married? Did she have any children? Was she dating someone? Whoever sent the roses certainly had a revelation coming if he thought the flowers would return him to Shauna's good graces. *It must be a boyfriend*, Kennedy concluded. She figured any husband of Shauna's would know better by now.

Unable to think of another scenario, Kennedy shook her head and tried to concentrate on her list once again. A few minutes later, Shauna breezed by Kennedy's desk. "I'm going to lunch."

Glancing at her wristwatch, Kennedy noticed it was way too early for lunch. She watched Shauna get into the elevator and knew her mind wouldn't rest until she satisfied her curiosity. Rising from her chair, Kennedy casually walked back to Shauna's office. She looked over her shoulder to make sure no one was watching, before bending down to the trash and grabbing the note tucked away in the flowers. Thankfully, the envelope wasn't sealed, so she quickly opened the card and scanned the note.

I'm sorry. I can't see you anymore. Please stop calling.

This was just perfect. It was no wonder Shauna was being more boorish than normal. She was in the middle of some lovers' spat. Hoping the two would make up quickly, Kennedy returned the note to the envelope and snuck out of the office, feeling mildly guilty for snooping.

✳ ✿ ✳

Unlocking the door with the spare key Braxton had lent her, Kennedy let herself into the third model home where she was greeted with the strong smell of fresh paint. The muted brown in the front room looked terrific with the bright white baseboards, casings, and crown molding. She slowly strolled through the rest of the main floor. What she saw pleased her immensely. She grabbed the light oak banister and followed the winding staircase upstairs. The master bedroom was lovely with deep burgundy paint; the office had turned out beautifully as well. The bathrooms looked quaint in sage green and light tan, and each of the extra bedrooms was a different charming shade of blue.

Making a mental note to call the painter with high praise, Kennedy continued on to the last bedroom and was met with a terrible surprise. What was supposed to be a pale yellow room was, instead, a sickly shade of pastel lavender. Not only was the color atrocious, but it would also completely clash with the fabric and theme they had chosen for the bedroom. Yanking her cell phone from her black leather handbag, Kennedy called the information number. Within a few minutes, she was being transferred to Professional Paint. She let the phone ring fifteen times before hanging up and shoving the phone back into her bag.

"Oh, fabulous," she groaned. "Now what am I going to do?" She knew how booked the painter's schedule was, and there wasn't much of a chance they could come back before the following week. The delay would throw off the schedule for the two remaining houses. What happened? How in the world could they have messed up with this one room? The painters were given such specific directions.

Just then the doorbell sounded, followed by two loud knocks. The furniture had arrived. Rushing down the stairs, Kennedy spent the next two hours directing the deliverymen where to put the furniture. With the exception of the ugly purple bedroom, all of the rooms were completely outfitted by the end of the afternoon. Kennedy made sure they left the last bedroom furniture just outside the door, lining the hallway.

Still pondering what to do about the paint problem, Kennedy glanced at her watch. It was 3:45. She decided to drive to the nearest home improvement store and purchase new paint and supplies, so she could do the job right herself. As she was locking up, she thought to check the garage for any extra painting supplies.

Though she didn't find any brushes or rollers, she did discover— much to her delight—the pale yellow paint that was meant to cover the walls. Hurrying outside, she jumped in her Corolla and raced as fast as she could in the thickening traffic to the home improvement store. Then she went on to her apartment, where she changed into some old faded blue sweats and grabbed her iPod and speakers.

She was back at the model home by five o'clock. Plugging in the speakers, she attached her iPod and cranked up the volume. It took her a good hour and a half to tape up the room and cover the floor in plastic. She had to keep reminding herself that she should be grateful it wasn't the master bedroom, or worse, the family room. At least it was one of the smallest rooms in the house. Thankfully, the walls didn't have too much texture, which made the painting go faster.

She quickly completed two walls and began rolling paint above the bedroom door—all the while singing along with her music. She stepped down from the barstool, loaded her roller with more paint, and climbed back up, pausing a moment to face the room and congratulate herself on her work. "Wow, I should be a professional. I'm good," she spoke aloud.

"But you've missed an entire wall." She jumped at the unexpected sound. Spinning around on the barstool, she nearly lost her balance but was quick to brace herself with the hand holding the roller. The only drawback was that the roller hit the wall hard, causing the fresh droplets of paint to scatter everywhere, landing primarily on Braxton's head and dark, tailored suit. Not knowing what to say, she stared down at him, completely aghast.

After surveying Kennedy's latest artwork on his relatively new suit, Braxton shook his head as he looked up at her. "Kennedy, I honestly don't know how to announce myself with you. I can't knock, because it results in you, and eventually me, being covered in flour. I can't call, because you don't recognize my voice and think you're meeting a stranger for lunch. And I can't just quietly walk into a room and say something, because I end up speckled with yellow paint."

"Well, at least it wasn't the ugly purple." She pointed at one wall still needing paint.

"What? No apologies?"

"You did startle me."

Rolling his eyes, he helped her down from the stool, asking, "Why are you repainting this room?"

"Because it's the wrong color."

"Oh," he responded, everything becoming clearer. "So you see it as your job to correct the work we are paying others to do?"

"Only when the 'others' won't be able to correct it themselves by the time I need it corrected."

Chuckling, Braxton shook his head again and grabbed the roller from Kennedy, intending to help her finish.

"No," she protested. "You'll get your suit even more covered."

"I doubt anyone will be able to get the paint out as it is."

"I really am so sorry." She bit her lip.

"No worries," he said, with his best Australian accent. "I can always get a new suit." He stripped off his jacket and dipped the roller, then climbed onto the barstool to paint where Kennedy had left off.

"You really don't need to help me. I'm almost done." After the flour incident, Kennedy knew it was useless to argue with him, so she meekly retrieved a paintbrush and started to paint the corner crevices where the roller wouldn't reach. "What are you doing here anyway?"

"Suzi called to say she needed me to sign something by tomorrow. She faxed it right over, but by the time I got around to reading and signing it, I called and realized she had already left for the day. So I just left a message on her voicemail that I would drop it by the model and leave it on the kitchen counter. I noticed your car outside and heard music blaring, so I thought I'd come investigate." He paused a moment, only to add with a smile, "Bad idea."

"I'll say," Kennedy agreed as her stomach growled loudly.

"I take it you haven't eaten dinner."

"No, and I'm starving."

"Good. Then I'll treat you to dinner when we're finished up here."

"But I'm the one who owes you dinner. Why don't you let it be my treat?"

"Have you forgotten that I get a home-cooked meal?"

"I guarantee you'll like what a restaurant has to offer better," she reasoned.

"You promised."

"Okay, okay," she said, caving. "How about Sunday night? That way, I might be able to convince my roommates to help."

Braxton was disappointed that she wanted to invite all her roommates. Perhaps he should have taken her up on the restaurant idea. "It's settled then. You cook me dinner on Sunday, and I take you to dinner tonight."

Braxton was making it sound like a date. Kennedy panicked

and stipulated, "Only so long as I can go home and change first." She hoped Stacey was home so they could invite her along.

"But you look beautiful," he told her truthfully.

She scoffed in disbelief. "Yeah, I'm thinking of entering the Miss America contest with this ensemble."

"Oh. Then maybe you could pass along a message to the current Miss America and tell her she owes me a date."

This time she laughed out loud. "I'll get right on it."

With Braxton's help, they finished quickly and cleaned up as much as they could. Braxton promised to drop by the next afternoon with another guy from work to help move in the remaining bedroom furnishings. After he heard Kennedy's stomach growl loudly again, he insisted they get fast food and eat in a park somewhere. That way, no one would be subjected to their paint-speckled attire.

Kennedy wasn't sure how she felt about being alone with Braxton now, considering he was becoming more and more likable each time that happened. But Braxton was adamant, and she was ravenous, so she reluctantly agreed.

He took her to In-N-Out and then to a nearby park. It was huge, and they had no trouble finding a place where they wouldn't be seen by too many people. After they situated themselves at the top of a small grassy hill overlooking a large pond, they dived into their burgers and french fries.

They ate in silence for a time before Braxton asked her a question. "So, why Arizona?"

She glanced at him quizzically. "I got a good job here."

"This was your only option?"

"No, not exactly. I got a few offers in some other locations."

"Where else?"

"Umm . . . ." Kennedy paused a moment to think. "Salt Lake City and Colorado Springs."

"Why didn't you take one of those? I thought you loved seasons."

"Oh, I would have loved either place, but it didn't feel right." Kennedy chewed her burger as she watched some ducks in the dimly lit pond.

"I see." He nodded thoughtfully, and then changed the subject. "So tell me, how did you make it though BYU still single?"

"Believe me, it wasn't too difficult," she said quickly, not liking where the conversation was headed.

"You didn't leave a boyfriend behind?" he asked.

Kennedy became quiet, wondering how to answer that question without lying. Finally, she shrugged nonchalantly. "Not really."

Braxton eyed her critically. He had hit a nerve, and the thought that it was about a past relationship made him lose his appetite a little. At first he thought of backing off, but, remembering her relentless questions about Crystal and his family, he opted to satisfy his curiosity. "What do you mean by 'not really'? You either did or you didn't."

"Excuse me?"

"Oh, don't act so shocked. After all, you personify meddling." Braxton finished his burger and leaned back on the grass, propping himself up with his arms. "How about we just start with a simple question?" He had to admit—it was pretty funny watching Kennedy squirm. "What was his name?"

"No," she protested. "No questions."

"Jeff? Seth? James? Matt?" He was unyielding. "Kelly? Warren? Tyler? Vernon?"

"Now you're being ridiculous." Kennedy allowed the corners of her mouth to turn up a little. "Like I would ever date anyone named Vernon."

"Hey, watch it." Braxton pointed a finger in her direction. "That was my grandfather's name."

"Oops, sorry."

"So, what was his name? Or do you want me to keep guessing?"

"Chris," she finally admitted reluctantly.

"That was going to be my next guess." He was glad to hear her laugh quietly. "So, where is this Chris now?"

"Oregon."

"Hmm . . . ," Braxton murmured, waiting for her to expound. After a few minutes had passed with no further explanation, he glanced over at her. "So, are you going to tell me the whole story, or do I have to painfully extract it from you question by question?"

She bit her lip, attempting to keep herself from smiling. "Well, you are good at asking nosy questions."

"Takes one to know one."

"Okay, okay," she acquiesced. "I'll tell you, but just keep in mind that you asked for it." Taking a deep breath, she began her personal narrative of heartbreak. "I was engaged to him," she said quietly. "We met our last year at BYU, dated for most of it, and got engaged in March. I had never clicked with anyone like I did with Chris. He was perfect for me, and I flattered myself into thinking I was perfect for him."

"He broke it off then?" Braxton questioned, not liking this story at all.

"No, I did." Kennedy's voice was barely a whisper.

Liking that answer better, Braxton couldn't keep from asking, "Why?"

"It wasn't right," she said, and shrugged simply. "I have no idea why, but for some reason it just wasn't." Braxton silently waited for her to continue. "It all began when we couldn't find a job near the same location. He got an incredible offer in Oregon, and Interior Essentials made me an offer that I felt good about. Finally, I decided it was more important to follow him to Oregon. But when I made that decision, I got this unsettling feeling and I just couldn't do it. So he decided to just move here with me, but that didn't feel right to me either. It was such a strange thing, and neither one of us could understand. I'll never forget the day that everything fell apart . . ." Kennedy's eyes got a faraway look as she remembered and attempted to relate the most difficult day of her life.

✳ ❀ ✳

"Cwistesen wesidence, dis is Mandy peaking." A small voice answered the phone.

Caught off guard, it took a second for Kennedy to realize that she had accidentally called her sister's home. She was sure that she had pressed Chris' speed dial button, but evidently she was mistaken. Jackie Christensen's four-year-old daughter had answered the phone. "Mandy! Hi! How are you? This is Aunt Kennedy!"

"Hi, Aunt Kendy!" Kennedy loved the way her niece pronounced her name. "Awe you coming to see us?" Mandy asked that every time Kennedy called. Jackie lived in Chicago where her husband worked for a large computer firm, so it was rare that Kennedy ever saw her sister.

"I would love to come visit you, Mandy! When can I come?" Kennedy smiled.

"Wight now!" Mandy said. "Pwease?"

Kennedy was about to say something else to her niece when she heard voices on the other end of the line, followed by her sister's voice on the phone. "Kennedy?"

"Hey, sis, how are you?"

"Oh, I'm great! I'm so happy you called!" Jackie said enthusiastically. "It seems like ages since I've talked to you. How are the wedding plans coming along?"

Not having the heart to tell her sister she had not meant to call her, Kennedy simply replied, "Well, now that they are off hold, I hope they will come along fine." It felt good to hear her sister's voice.

"What do you mean off hold? Did you change the date or something?"

Kennedy had forgotten Jackie knew nothing of her indecisiveness. Not wanting to get into a long explanation with her sister, she replied quickly, "Oh, I was having some confusing feelings, but I think I've finally made a decision, so the plans are back on."

"You think?" Jackie questioned.

"No." Kennedy forced a chuckle. "I know."

"What confusing feelings?"

Kennedy took a deep breath. She should have known her sister would not rest until she knew everything. "I don't know for sure, Jack. I think the stress of job hunting, in addition to the stress of the wedding, just threw some confusing emotions my way."

"Oh," her sister said slowly. "So, you're feeling better now? You said you finally made a decision?"

"Well, yeah, I think so. I decided to forget about my offer in Arizona and go to Oregon with Chris to find a job there."

"And you feel good about that decision?"

Kennedy hesitated. "Yeah."

"Are you sure?"

Suddenly, Kennedy felt a rush of emotions come over her, and she resisted the urge to start crying in frustration. "Oh, I don't know. I thought so, but now you're making me wonder all over again," her voice quivered as she spoke the words.

"Hey, Kenn, I didn't mean to upset you." Jackie's concern was evident. When Kennedy didn't reply, she continued, "Are you okay? You don't sound so good."

That was too much for Kennedy. She hadn't talked to anyone about her feelings lately, but something in her sister's voice caused all Kennedy's emotions to surface. She felt an irresistible urge to open up to her sister and began to pour out all of her frustrations. She told her sister about everything—from the initial offer letter from Phoenix to her conversations with Chris. Jackie quietly listened until Kennedy finished with the words, "I finally decided to move to Oregon, but I still have an unsettling feeling that won't go away. I just don't understand what I'm supposed to do." Kennedy waited for her sister's comforting words, but she only heard silence on the other end. "Jack, are you there?"

"Yeah, I'm still here, Kenn."

"Well, what do you think about all this?"

"I'm not sure if you want to know what I think."

"Why not?"

"Frankly, Kennedy, from everything you've told me, it sounds to me like maybe you aren't listening. Has it ever occurred to you that you're taking the wrong question to the Lord? You said you both feel at peace with your respective job offers, but they are in different locations." Jackie paused before saying quietly, "For me, that would definitely be a red flag. Kenn, as hard as it may be, have you ever decided not to marry Chris to see how you feel once you've made that decision?"

Kennedy willed herself not to be offended by her sister's comments. Instead, she answered honestly, "No, I haven't. I don't think the Lord would want to stop me from marrying someone as wonderful as Chris. He will be an amazing husband and father. Family is the most important thing in this life. Why would Heavenly Father stop me from reaching such an important goal?"

"Oh, I'm sure He doesn't want to stop you, Kennedy," her sister said calmly and quietly. Kennedy breathed a sigh of relief until Jackie continued, "Maybe He just wants to postpone it for awhile."

Kennedy felt chills surge through her body as her sister uttered the words. The rightness of Jackie's comments sank deep into Kennedy's heart, causing a wrenching pain. Suddenly, everything became glaringly clear in Kennedy's mind. For the first time, she seriously examined the possibility that perhaps she shouldn't marry Chris—at least not yet. As the dreaded thought entered her mind, Kennedy felt immersed in peace. An unseen weight lifted from her shoulders, and she knew that the Lord had answered her prayers. It was the most horrible, disappointing, and bittersweet confirmation she could have asked for. She felt as though her heart were ripping in two. Nearly dropping the phone, Kennedy sank to the floor in anguish.

"Kennedy?" her sister's voice rang distantly. "Are you there?"

It took a moment for Kennedy to gather herself. "Yeah, I'm still here," she said shakily, as a tear cascaded down her cheek. Wiping the moisture from her face, Kennedy continued. "I actually have a confession to make, Jackie. When I picked up the phone a half an hour ago, it wasn't to call you. I meant to push Chris's speed dial button—not yours. I'm not sure how it happened that your phone rang, but I know why now." Kennedy took a deep breath. "Thanks, Jack. As difficult as it's going to be, I know what I need to do now."

Jackie's voice was filled with pain. "Are you going to be okay, sis?"

"Yeah." Kennedy nodded sadly, wanting to hang up the phone before her emotions erupted. "I'll be fine."

It wasn't until after Kennedy hung up the phone, ran to her room, and threw herself onto her bed, that she let the torrents of tears come. So many thoughts raced through her mind. How was she going to do this? How could Chris not be the right one for her? How could she live without him? How would she tell him, and how was he going to react? Would their paths cross somewhere down the road, or would they go their separate ways forever? But the most unrelenting question that would continue to plague her was, why?

Unable to bear the pain any longer, Kennedy turned to the only sure source of comfort she knew. Sinking to the floor, she began the most fervent prayer she had ever said. Pouring out her heart to her Father in Heaven, she prayed for comfort, for strength, and for understanding. An hour later, she arose slowly, her eyes swollen and red. Noticing her scriptures lying next to the bed on the floor, she picked them up. A renewed sense of peace and calm filled her soul as she read the words, "all these things shall give thee experience, and shall be for thy good." Kennedy finished the last two verses of the chapter, closed the book, and went to the phone to dial Chris's number once again.

✳ ✿ ✳

Kennedy still missed Chris a great deal, but she found it much easier to talk and think about him now that she was beginning to feel something for someone else. For the duration of her account, Braxton sat there patiently, listening to every word. She finally concluded by explaining, "And I haven't heard from him since."

"Wow," was all Braxton could think to say. "That is quite a story."

"You can't say I didn't warn you."

Braxton chuckled as he slowly got to his feet. He reached for her hand and pulled her up beside him, without relinquishing his hold on her hand. "It took a lot of faith to do what you did."

His touch sent a delightful shiver through her body. Kennedy stared into his gorgeous blue eyes, completely entranced. Finally, she blinked and looked away in embarrassment. *He likes Stacey. He likes Stacey. He likes Stacey. And Stacey is in love with him.* She had to keep reminding herself. "Well, now that my life is an open book, I should probably get going." She quickly pulled her hand from his grip, unsettled by the way he was making her feel.

Braxton silently gathered up the empty sacks before they walked back toward the truck. As he opened the passenger door to let her in, he made a suggestion. "Hey, you look pretty worn out, and we're closer to your apartment than we are to the model home. Why don't I just drive you back to your place and then pick you up in the morning?"

"Sounds fine to me." She nodded her agreement as she sat down, realizing how exhausted she was. "But in order to be fair, I have to warn you that we planned on meeting at the model home at six-thirty tomorrow morning."

He closed the door and walked around to the other side. "You know, that information might have been good to know before I made the suggestion to pick you up," he said wryly. "Now I'm going to sound like a cad if I suddenly change my mind."

"That's probably true," she agreed with a smile. He glared across the car at her, so she quickly amended, "But don't let me stop you from being a cad."

Chuckling, he started the car and drove her back to her apartment, attempting to change her mind about the early meeting time. As he pulled up to her place, she jumped out immediately. "Thanks so much for the ride," she said brightly. "I'll see you a little after six tomorrow morning!" Then she slammed the door before he could utter a response.

Braxton waited for a minute to make sure she made it inside, shaking his head at her retreating figure. When she waved a final good-bye and closed the door behind her, he suddenly felt very alone. He realized that he was already missing Kennedy Jackson even though he would see her again in just a few more hours. Rolling his eyes, he turned his truck around and headed home mumbling, "Braxton, you are pathetic."

❊ Chapter 10 ❊

S UNDAY AFTERNOON FOUND Kennedy in a cooking frenzy. Knowing she should have shadowed her mother in the kitchen more during her youth only increased her stress. She decided to make the only dish she had ever been complimented on—lasagna. Of course, the compliment did come from her encouraging mother, but when it came to her cooking skills—or lack thereof—Kennedy took what she could get.

Mia had to work that night, and Becca had been invited to Jason's apartment, so it would just be herself and Stacey. If it weren't for the fact that she was in charge of cooking, Kennedy would definitely have found someplace else to be. As it was, she felt like a third wheel with Stacey and Braxton and wished once more that Becca or Mia could be there.

Stacey had helped to make a salad earlier, but had gone to meet with a study group for a couple of hours before Braxton arrived. She left Kennedy to finish up in the kitchen while she ran out the door in a frenzy.

Kennedy was buttering the French bread when she caught a whiff of something burning. Dropping the knife, she dove for the oven and wrenched open the door. Smoke billowed out, and she was dismayed to see her lasagna bubbling over onto the oven floor. She watched helplessly as the smoke and a foul burnt odor permeated the room, followed by the distinct and humiliating shriek of the smoke detector.

Of course, Braxton chose that moment to let himself in. He didn't even bother to knock when he heard the fire alarm. It echoed louder than any pounding he could administer. Finding Kennedy rushing about, opening windows, and turning on the ceiling fans, Braxton couldn't help but laugh. "At least the sprinklers didn't go off," he said, pointing at the ceiling. "Yet."

"I told you a restaurant would be better!" she exclaimed crossly, as she pulled open a window.

"You can't seriously pin the blame for this on me. I walked in after the fire alarm went off, remember?"

"You wanted a home-cooked meal. Any idiot in their right mind would take one look at me and know that I am not a cook!" she cried.

"Well, you're so good at everything else, one naturally assumes that you'd be a good cook as well." Chuckling under his breath, he gently moved Kennedy out of the way, opened the oven door, and peered inside. He removed the lasagna and set it on a nearby cookie sheet. Once the majority of the mess at the bottom of the oven was scooped out with a spatula, he returned the lasagna and cookie sheet back into the oven, preventing any additional leakage from burning.

"Well, it looks like the hero saved the day," Kennedy said wryly as she sank, exhausted, into a nearby chair. "Thanks, Brax."

"You're welcome," he replied graciously, grabbing the knife off the counter and buttering the rest of the bread. Once he was finished, he rifled through their sparse spice cabinet, pulled out a couple of spices, and began shaking them over the top of the bread.

"What are you doing to my bread?" Kennedy jumped up and came to stand beside him, reaching to take the spices from him.

"I'm giving it some flavor." He elbowed her out of the way as he finished. "Trust me, you'll love this."

"Please don't tell me you moonlight as a chef during your time off," she muttered as she plopped back down at the table.

"No, it's just a hobby." Braxton pulled out a chair, turned it around backwards, and sat down beside her. "So, you can't cook," he mused. "Is there anything else you can't do that I should know about?"

Kennedy laughed. "Loads. Let's see . . . I can't sing, as you are well aware, I can't ride a bike with no hands, and in all the times I've gone fishing, I've never caught one fish. I can't slalom ski—I always fishtail out of control—I can't fly a kite, I can't tell a good joke, I can't run more than a mile without dying, and I can't make a batch of cookies without burning at least one pan. But, the ones that don't get burned taste fabulous!" She smiled broadly. "I figured I'd end with a positive."

Braxton laughed out loud.

"Now, what about you? What can't you do?"

Braxton appeared thoughtful before answering, "Nothing that I can think of."

Kennedy threw a hot pad at him. "I should have known you'd say that."

"So, tell me about your home and family." Braxton changed the subject.

"Mmm, that's an easy one." Thoughts of her family made her smile. "My parents are incredible. They're kind, supportive, and they both have a great sense of humor. My father owns a sporting goods store in Albuquerque, and he is obsessed with golfing. My mom loves Scrabble, cooking, and gardening. She has the most beautiful yard in our neighborhood.

"I have four siblings who are all married and scattered around the country. Jackie and her husband, Kevin, live in Chicago with their three children. Aaron and his wife, Karla, live in Massachusetts and have one on the way. Kyla lives with her husband, Mike, in Colorado. They have two kids. And Josh is going to physical therapy school in Kentucky with his wife, Becky. I'm really looking forward to Christmas this year. Kyla and her family usually come because they live the closest, but this year Jackie and her family are flying out as well. I can't wait."

Braxton nodded thoughtfully. "That's great."

Kennedy reached across the table and covered his hand with her own. She searched his face sympathetically. "I'm sorry, Brax. I didn't mean to remind you—"

"I wanted to know," he interrupted. "So, did you make me any of those fabulous cookies you talked about?"

"Yes, and believe it or not, I didn't burn one of them." She grinned as she leaned back, removing her hand from his.

"Only the dinner then?"

"The lasagna isn't burnt, it just—oh, no!" she yelped, jumping up from the table and running to the oven.

"I'm back!" Stacey entered the apartment, tossing her backpack on the nearest chair. Wrinkling her nose, she sniffed the air and pulled out a chair next to Braxton. "What's that smell?"

✳ ✿ ✳

"What are you doing?" Suzi asked, walking up to stand beside Kennedy and watching her rifle through a stack of papers piled high on her desk.

"It's the strangest thing," Kennedy said. "You remember the room with the lavender paint?"

"How could I forget?"

"Well, I just got off the phone with Professional Paint and they said they received a change order with my signature at the bottom. I know that things are crazy right now, and I did make a few last minute changes, but lavender has never been planned for any of the homes. I'm just trying to find a copy of the change order the painter was talking about." Kennedy continued to sift through the papers as she asked, "You or Katie didn't happen to make any changes did you?"

"I didn't," Suzi replied. "And I can't imagine Katie did either. Dealing with the painter was your job."

"I know, I know. I'm sure I just messed up." Kennedy sighed in frustration, pushing aside the papers. "I'm just going to call and ask them to fax me over a copy."

"All right, but once you've satisfied your curiosity, do you mind meeting me at my desk? I have a couple of things I'd like to run by you."

"Sure," Kennedy said as she picked up the receiver. "I'll be over as soon as I get off the phone."

"Thanks."

A couple of hours later, Kennedy checked the fax machine and found the change order from the painter. Sure enough, her signature was at the bottom. Only, it wasn't hers. Not exactly. The *k* wasn't slanted quite enough, the *y* had an extra tiny flourish, and the *i* was a little large. It was a forgery. But who would do such a thing? Suzi and Katie had signed for Kennedy many times, but their handwriting didn't even come close to Kennedy's. This one was obviously practiced. But why, and by who? Would Shauna have sunk this low, hoping to put a kink in Kennedy's tight-knit schedule? She couldn't imagine anyone else forging her name.

Knowing she'd go crazy if she continued to worry about it, Kennedy forced her mind back to what she needed to accomplish that day. She had too much on her plate to spend any more time on this mystery. Besides, she had no way of proving anything, and she had a lot of phone calls to make.

Over the course of the next week, Kennedy was so busy with work that she was able to put the paint mishap from her mind—at least partially. They were able to finish decorating the fourth home, and everything was on schedule for the final model to be finished the following week. That is, until another problem surfaced.

Kennedy had arrived at the last model home one afternoon, planning to meet the furniture delivery trucks. She waited three hours before finally calling the company, only to discover that they received a phone call earlier that morning, asking to delay the delivery until after Christmas. Kennedy quickly told them they'd need to reschedule as soon as possible, but, unfortunately, the soonest they could fit it into their schedule was still five days away on Christmas Eve. Trying to remain calm, Kennedy scheduled the delivery, asking them to please call should they have an opening before then. Making sure that the delivery was set in stone, regardless of any more mystery phone calls they might receive, she left the model home completely irate.

Slamming the door behind her, Kennedy stalked into the apartment, her eyes blazing. She found the front room already occupied by Stacey—and Braxton, no less. She grimaced and immediately made a beeline for her bedroom. She wasn't exactly in the mood to talk to anyone, much less tell Braxton that they were now officially behind schedule.

"Whoa, what's got you all shook up?" Braxton was obviously fearless.

"Nothing." Kennedy stormed past them and slammed her bedroom door behind her. She began pacing back and forth like a caged animal, trying to calm down and find a solution for the damage that had been done. Nothing came to mind. They couldn't finish decorating until the furniture was in place, and the furniture would not be in place until Christmas Eve. Then it would take an additional day to finish the decorating. Kennedy didn't know what to do. Not only did Katie and Suzi already have flights booked to see their families, but Kennedy had also promised her own family she'd be home for Christmas. She would be beyond depressed if she had to break her promise.

The models had already been advertised to open up New Year's Day, so the only other option was to come back the day after Christmas and finish all of the decorating alone—since she wasn't about the ask Suzi and Katie to fly back early. Seeing this as a depressing but viable option, Kennedy finally began to calm down somewhat. She began to make a mental list of everything she could do before the furniture arrived. If she had everything organized, it would only take a day or two for her to finish the decorating by herself. That way, she'd be able to extend her visit home a little longer.

About thirty minutes later, a light tapping sounded on her door. "Come in," Kennedy called absentmindedly, still pacing as she continued to sort things out in her mind.

Braxton poked his head through the door. "Is it safe?" he joked.

Ignoring his teasing, Kennedy flopped down on her bed in exhaustion. "Where's Stace?"

Letting himself in, Braxton pulled out the desk chair, and sat down on it backwards. "I think she's afraid of you at the moment," he said, smiling. Kennedy glared. "Actually, she had to take a test tonight, or at least that's the excuse she gave me. I'm thinking she's not one for uncomfortable situations, so I'm sure she was more than happy to flee the apartment. In fact, she tried to convince me to leave too."

"Smart girl," Kennedy said. "You would've been wise to follow her lead." She still didn't want to tell Braxton about what happened, but he would find out soon enough. She decided to get it over with. "There's been a slight setback in our schedule," she said. "We won't be finished before Christmas, but your homes will still be ready to open up on New Year's Day."

Braxton furrowed his brow. "But I thought you were almost finished. Are you telling me that you plan to work through the holidays?"

"Yes, and yes." Kennedy said dejectedly, explaining what had happened with the furniture delivery as well as the reason for the paint mishap. When she was finished, Braxton looked upset.

"Why didn't you tell me about the paint earlier?"

"What could you have done?"

"Believe me, I would have done something. I can't believe Shauna would have the temerity—"

"We don't know that it was Shauna," Kennedy interrupted.

"Oh please, who else would it be?" Braxton raked his fingers through his hair in anger.

Kennedy had to laugh as she watched him. "It's a good thing Stacey's not around to see this."

"This is not funny, Kenn." Braxton stopped to look at her intently. "You cannot let Shauna get away with this."

"What am I supposed to do? Confront her tomorrow morning and tell her she's a nincompoop? Maybe I could threaten her with a lawsuit. Oh wait, that would require some sort of proof. Or perhaps we could go and toilet-paper her house tonight. That would show her." Kennedy was giggling now.

"Please stop before I have you committed." Braxton grinned as he stepped in front of her and grabbed her shoulders, crouching down so that he was eye-level with her. "What I meant is that you can't let her mess up your schedule or the holidays."

"It's too late for that." Kennedy was finding it difficult to breathe regularly.

"I disagree."

"I'm all ears," Kennedy said.

Smiling, he retracted his hands, stood, and headed for the door. "I've got a few phone calls to make. Just be at the model home tomorrow by one."

"Wait!" Kennedy yelped, jumping up to follow him. "You can't leave me hanging like that. I'll be up all night wondering."

"Take a sleeping pill." He smiled as he shut the apartment door behind him.

✳ ✿ ✳

Kennedy was eating a sandwich on the steps of the model home the following afternoon when she caught sight of Braxton's truck heading down the street. Followed by another truck . . . and another . . . and another . . . and another. The last truck was pulling a gigantic trailer. Each truck was packed with furniture—her furniture! Or rather, the furniture for the model home. Kennedy couldn't believe it. She leaped up in delight, dropping her forgotten sandwich on the steps.

Braxton was just jumping out of his truck when he spotted Kennedy running toward him. Before he could say a word, she had thrown herself in his arms, hugging him tightly. "I can't believe it! You're amazing! How did you arrange all this?"

Braxton laughed, thinking he needed to ingratiate himself much more often if this was her way of saying thanks. "Let's just say I know a few guys with trucks."

"I'll say!" Kennedy exclaimed, pulling free from his arms and smiling broadly at all the trucks. She was so happy, she felt like crying.

Braxton quickly introduced everyone and then turned to Kennedy. "So where do you want all this stuff?"

✳ ✿ ✳

Thanks to Braxton, and with the hard-working help of Suzi and Katie, they were able to finish decorating the final home exactly one day after their original deadline, making it possible for everyone to enjoy their holidays as planned.

After hanging up the last picture on the family room wall, the three collapsed on a nearby sofa, reveling in the satisfaction of the completed project.

"I can't believe it!" squealed Katie as she surveyed the home. "We actually finished, and I have to say—it looks awesome! If I had the money, I'd move into one of these homes in a minute!"

Kennedy grinned at Katie's enthusiasm. "Well, I've got to hand it to you both. I couldn't have done it without you. You are two very talented girls."

"Oh, go on." Suzi waved off Kennedy's comment with a laugh. "You're the talented one. We just did what you told us to do."

Kennedy rolled her eyes, belying Suzi's praise. "Now, who's up for some frozen custard?" She sprang from the couch and rushed for the front door. "Last one to the car has to pay!" she called back. Katie and Suzi followed in hot pursuit. Flinging open the front door, Kennedy ran into a beautiful woman in her early forties. Neither Katie nor Suzi could stop in time, and they both careened into Kennedy, forcing Kennedy forward and pushing the woman into Braxton.

"Oh my goodness. I am so sorry, Caroline." Kennedy apologized to the woman the moment she regained her balance. "We were racing to my car and had no idea anyone was out here."

"That's all right." Caroline smiled, straightening out her navy blue business suit. "No harm done. We were just stopping by to see how you were making out." Caroline was the head interior designer for Taylor Homes—a talented woman who Kennedy had gotten to know from their brief conversations throughout the past few months. Caroline had an engaging, easy-going personality, and Kennedy had felt immediately comfortable around her. She had given Kennedy great advice without making her feel like a greenie. Caroline was the kind of person Kennedy wished she could find in Shauna.

"You are too nice, Caroline." Kennedy grinned. "If someone were to run me over like that, I'd definitely tell them where to go."

"I'll vouch for that," Braxton cut in before Caroline could utter a response. Then, ignoring Kennedy's glare, he quickly introduced Caroline to Suzi and Katie.

"I've heard so much about you two from Kennedy," Caroline gushed. "In fact, I'd hire you in a minute based on her recommendations of you." Katie and Suzi both blushed at the compliment.

Kennedy smiled at her co-workers before turning back to Caroline and Braxton. "I have to say that you have impeccable timing. We were actually on our way out for ice cream to celebrate." Kennedy stepped aside and grinned, waving them all back inside. "We are finished!" Catching Braxton's arm as he walked by, Kennedy gave it a quick squeeze and whispered, "Thanks to you!"

The five of them spent the next few hours going through each of the model homes, surveying all of Kennedy's, Suzi's, and Katie's hard work. Caroline and Braxton praised and complimented every room they were shown. After the tour was completed, Caroline jokingly offered them each a job, with Braxton seconding her opinion. They both had meetings to get to, so they waved a final good-bye and left Kennedy, Suzi, and Katie free to get their celebratory ice cream.

❁ Chapter 11 ❁

B. J.!" STACEY EXCLAIMED, an engaging smile forming on her lips. "This is a surprise. Come on in." Her heart skipped a beat as she ushered him inside, taking note of the two gift bags he was carrying. It was a late Wednesday afternoon, and Stacey was home alone studying for her last final. Becca had finished a day earlier and had already left to stay at her family's house for Christmas. Mia was working overtime through the holidays, trying to save as much as she could before she quit her job in a couple of weeks to start school. Kennedy had left early that morning to drive to New Mexico to be with her family until after New Year's.

Stacey was feeling completely alone when B. J. surprised her by showing up at the apartment. She had been meaning to call and invite him to her family's home for Christmas but had been so busy with finals that she hadn't gotten around to phoning him. She figured it was no big deal though, considering he had spent the last two Christmases with her family, so of course he would be planning to come again this year. "I've been meaning to call you B. J., to see if you wanted to spend Christmas with our family again. You know you're always invited."

"You and your family are the best, Stace." He smiled fondly at her, not noticing the slight blush that touched her cheeks. He casually leaned against the counter, tossing the gift bags on top. "Normally, you know I would be there—I consider you family, you know, but I actually have to head over to New Mexico to deal with a couple of problems that have arisen with our new development."

Stacey looked away quickly, trying desperately not to show her disappointment. "But what will you do for Christmas?"

"I'm not worried about that," he drawled, glancing around as if looking for someone. "You know me and holidays."

"Yeah, I do," she responded quietly, looking down at her shoes. "Well, we'll miss you."

Braxton smiled kindly, once again glancing past Stacey. His eyes roamed a minute and finally landed on the gift bags he had brought. "Oh, that reminds me . . ." He grabbed the smaller of the two bags and held it out to her. "I have a gift for your family."

"You didn't have to do that, B. J." She smiled warmly.

"I know, but like I said, you guys are the only family I have." He grinned and nodded toward the bag. "Go ahead. Open it."

She didn't need to be told twice and quickly opened the bag to find a huge box of chocolates. "Ooh, yummy!" She grinned. "My family will love these!" She threw her arms around him. "Thanks."

Braxton hugged her back and smiled. "No thanks necessary, Stace." He quickly released her and took one more glance over her shoulder before asking, "Hey, is Kennedy around?"

He didn't notice Stacey's eyes glaze over, nor did he catch a drop in her enthusiasm. "No," Stacey said nonchalantly. "She left this morning to go home for the holidays."

"Oh." He mentally kicked himself for not coming over the night before. Grabbing the larger gift bag off the counter, he headed for the door, smiling back at Stacey. "I suppose this will have to wait until after the holidays then." Opening the door, he said, "I hope you have a great Christmas, Stace."

Stacey pasted a smile on her face until the door closed behind him. "Fat chance." Glumly, she opened the box of chocolates and popped a large caramel into her mouth, wishing Kennedy Jackson had never moved to Arizona.

❋ ❋ ❋

Kennedy pulled up to her parents' home feeling a mixture of excitement and sadness. She couldn't wait to see her parents and the two of her sisters that were going to be there with their families, but she also knew she would miss her roommates and friends from her ward—not to mention Braxton. Thoughts of him lowered her boisterous spirits. She would miss seeing and working with him, but it was definitely for the best. Kennedy needed to distance herself, and the Christmas break was a good start. What better way to get her mind off someone who was way out of her reach than to spend a couple weeks with her beloved family? Once the holidays were over, she would have to go back to seeing and conversing with her she-devil of a supervisor every day. The contemplation did nothing to bolster her spirits, so she cast the image of Shauna aside and thought only of her family and the fun couple of weeks ahead instead.

It was wonderful to see her parents, Jackie, Kyla, and their families, and Kennedy was more than happy to reacquaint herself with Jackie's three children—Anna, Mandy, and Jacob—and Kyla's two—Byron and Jessica. She adored her nieces and nephews and prayed that one day they would all live in the same place so their children could grow up together.

On Christmas Eve morning, Kennedy woke up with the familiar excitement Christmas always brought. Smelling the enticing aroma of blueberry muffins, she forgot all about a shower and immediately followed her nose to the kitchen where her two sisters were seated at the bar, eating muffins.

"Hey, sis," Kyla said as Kennedy entered the room. "Somehow I knew this smell would wake you."

Kennedy laughed as she pulled up a third barstool next to her sisters and grabbed the closest muffin. "You did this on purpose," she accused.

Jackie quipped, "Well, since you don't have children to wake you up at insane hours, we thought we'd do the job."

"Just be grateful we chose a kinder approach than our children do," teased Kyla.

"Well, regardless of the reason, thank you." Kennedy savored her muffin. "I love blueberry muffins."

"We know," her sisters chimed in unison.

"So, how are you doing, Kenn?" Jackie asked carefully. This was the first time that she had been alone with her sisters since she arrived home.

Knowing exactly what Jackie was referring to, Kennedy gave a small smile and answered honestly. "I'm doing really well, actually." She thoughtfully picked apart another muffin before continuing. "I still miss Chris, and I think I'll always wonder why he wasn't right for me, but I'm at peace with my decision, and I am really enjoying Arizona."

"Yeah, Mom tells us you're working for some Mr. Perfect," Kyla said in a teasing tone.

"Mr. Perfect?" Kennedy laughed. "Mom did not say that."

"Okay, okay." Her sister smiled. "She said a nice young man. But she seemed to think that you were starting to have some feelings for him."

Kennedy blushed lightly at her sister's frankness. Her cheeks turned a shade darker when her two sisters smiled knowingly at each other. Not one to lie, Kennedy rolled her eyes and decided to set the story straight. "Braxton is a very nice guy and, yes, I do like him a lot, but the job I did for him is now over, and I doubt I'll see much of him in the future. Besides, he and my roommate Stacey supposedly have some sort of relationship going on."

"Supposedly?" Jackie queried.

"Yes," replied Kennedy. "I'm not around that much when he comes over, but from what Becca says, Stacey and Braxton should be engaged any day now."

"But you obviously seem to think differently," Kyla observed.

"I used to think that he did, but now I wonder if he's just so nice that he inadvertently makes people think he cares more than he really does—if that makes sense." Kennedy hesitated a moment before explaining, "They've never really dated, and he doesn't treat her any differently than the rest of us."

Her sisters nodded their understanding as Jackie asked, "So, you don't think he feels anything for you above friendship?"

Shaking her head, Kennedy replied quickly, "No, thank goodness. Stacey would never forgive me."

"Well, his loss," Kyla said simply. Jackie smiled, and Kennedy giggled.

Just then the doorbell rang, and Kennedy heard a loud pounding of little feet above her head as her nieces and nephews all raced down the stairs to answer it. Kyla and Jackie were up in a flash and demanded that their children stop at once. Five little faces stopped and looked solemnly up at their moms.

"Where are your manners?" Jackie questioned sternly. "You don't want to scare our visitor off now, do you?" Five little heads shook in unison.

Kennedy emerged from the kitchen, with another partially eaten muffin in her hand. Smiling at her nieces and nephews, she said, "Well, if no one is going to get the door, I think that'll effectively get rid of the visitor as well. And quite frankly, if it were me at the door, I would rather be scared than ignored." She crouched down to the kids' eye level. "I say you go scare him."

Five pairs of eyes shone with delight as they once again headed to the front door and flung it wide open.

Jackie glared at Kennedy. "Do you realize you just undermined our parental authority?"

Popping the last of the muffin into her mouth, Kennedy only smiled. She spun around to welcome the visitor, and her heart stopped. There, standing just inside the door, was Braxton Taylor. Kennedy was speechless. Noting her sister's expression, Jackie studied Braxton with open curiosity.

Braxton spoke. "Somehow it doesn't surprise me that Kennedy would undermine someone's parental authority." He grinned at Jackie and Kyla as he extended his hand. "Hi, I'm Braxton Taylor. I'm a friend of Kennedy's from Arizona." He crouched down toward the children. "And you must be some of the many nieces and nephews she adores. Thanks for letting me in."

The children all laughed but soon decided that the excitement was over and raced back upstairs to continue their play.

Kyla was first to find her voice. "Hi, Braxton. I'm Kyla, and this is Jackie." She gestured toward her sister. "Kennedy was just telling us about the project she did for you."

Braxton smiled at Kennedy. "Yes, and I must say that you have a talented sister. You should see the homes she decorated."

Kennedy finally shook the cobwebs from her head, swallowed the remains of the muffin in one large gulp, and didn't bother hiding her surprise. "Brax, what are you doing here?" Her face was flushed with embarrassment as she berated herself for not showering and changing before coming down for breakfast.

"I was in the neighborhood and thought I'd come say hello."

"You have family in this area too?" Jackie questioned.

"No, actually I've been in Albuquerque overseeing a development for the past couple of days. I was just on my way back to Arizona and thought I'd drop by." He smiled and picked up the gift bag he had brought. "Besides, Kennedy left town without her Christmas present." He handed the bag to a, once again, speechless Kennedy.

Jackie and Kyla exchanged knowing glances. "Braxton, would you like some blueberry muffins?" Kyla questioned. "That is, unless Kennedy has eaten them all."

"I'd love some." Braxton grinned. "I'm starving."

"Great!" Jackie exclaimed. "Well, how about you come with us to the kitchen, and we'll let Kennedy go and freshen up a bit."

"What are you saying, Jack?" Kennedy couldn't help saying as she grabbed the gift bag from Braxton and quickly made her escape.

Twenty minutes later, Kennedy had showered and changed into a pair of boot-cut jeans and a pale pink sweater. Her hair was still slightly damp, but at that point she was more worried about the damage her sisters could be doing than she was about her hair. She rushed down the stairs and back into the kitchen to find Kyla pulling a new batch of muffins from the oven. The three of them were laughing and chatting like they were old friends.

"Hey, sis," Kyla said as Kennedy arrived.

Braxton turned around and pulled out the barstool next to him, gesturing for her to take a seat. Cautiously, she slid in beside him. "Since when did you become so social?" she asked.

"Since today," was all he said.

"Well, I forgot to thank you before," Kennedy said lamely.

"For what?" He looked a little perplexed.

"The gift."

"Oh, did you like it?"

"I don't know."

Braxton shrugged. "Well, maybe it will grow on you."

Kyla and Jackie stifled giggles while Kennedy rolled her eyes and explained, "I meant that I haven't opened it yet. It's not Christmas."

"Ah," he grinned. "You're one of those kind of people."

"Kennedy takes Christmas very seriously, Braxton," Kyla explained. "You see, only small white lights can be hung on the Christmas tree, and the ornaments must be arranged perfectly. Hot chocolate must be made every night for two weeks prior, and it must be enjoyed with a Christmas story. Christmas music has to be played constantly after Thanksgiving, and—most important—Christmas presents can only be opened on Christmas."

"Oh, hush," Kennedy responded with a smile. "I don't know why they love to tease me so much. And speaking of teasing, where are Mike and Kevin?"

"They're over at the church playing basketball," Jackie replied. "So, Braxton, how long are you here for?"

"Not long," he said. "I'd better get going soon."

"Are you spending Christmas with Stacey and her family?" Kennedy asked.

"Actually, no," he said. "I thought I'd be in Albuquerque a lot longer."

"Oh, so why do you have to head back so soon?" inquired Kennedy.

"I have some stuff to do at the office."

"On Christmas?" Kennedy was horrified.

"Yeah."

"Braxton!" Kennedy exclaimed. "CEO or not, you can't work on Christmas!" She looked at her sisters imploringly.

"Great! I guess it's settled then." Jackie came to her rescue first. "You'll just have to spend Christmas with us."

"No, I really have to get back."

"Listen to me, Braxton, we are doing you a huge favor by inviting you." Kyla leaned in closer and grinned. "After all, you will never hear the end of it if you spend Christmas working. You should have stretched the truth if you really wanted to escape unscathed."

"For once, my sister speaks the truth." Kennedy smiled and rose from the counter. "Now, where are your bags? Let's get you settled."

Braxton followed Kennedy outside. "Kenn, I really do need to head back. I certainly didn't stop by to finagle some invitation from you and your family."

"No one said you did. And you are more than welcome to leave the day after Christmas." Kennedy had reached his truck and grabbed his bag from the cab before heading back inside. "Besides, like Jackie said, you shouldn't have told me you didn't have plans, because now I don't feel the least bit guilty." She grinned as she threw his duffle bag on the bed in the last spare bedroom upstairs. She was lucky that her sister's families preferred the basement. Noticing the troubled look on his face, Kennedy tried a different argument. "Besides, I'd really like it if you stayed."

Braxton lifted his shoulders in a gesture of defeat. "All right, you win."

Kennedy smiled broadly and threw her arms around him in an impulsive hug. "I'm so glad! You will have so much fun!"

Braxton chuckled as he hugged her back.

As she pulled back, her eyes locked with his, and she realized she had made a monumental mistake when she'd insisted that he stay. In a moment of distraction, she'd forgotten her resolve to get over the feelings she was beginning to have for him. It felt so good to be in his arms. He was so good, kind, witty, brilliant, and wonderful. How could she not care for him? Breaking eye contact, she pulled away, feeling self-conscience and at a loss for words.

Braxton gently took her arm and led her back down the stairs. Not a word was spoken, but Kennedy knew that her spontaneous hug was more than friendly. She had crossed some imaginary line, all because she was an impetuous fool, and that knowledge frightened her a great deal.

Kennedy's parents had returned from the store, and her brothers-in-law were back from playing basketball. After a quick introduction, Braxton was treated like one of the family. They spent the afternoon talking, laughing, and eating. Olivia made a huge Christmas Eve dinner, and afterward Kennedy's nieces and nephews dressed up and acted out the first Christmas story. Finally, the evening culminated with hot chocolate. Once Kennedy had passed around mugs filled with the steamy liquid, she paused to survey her beloved family celebrating this special holiday. Feeling Braxton's breath on her neck, Kennedy wasn't startled when she heard him say quietly, "A penny for your thoughts."

Smiling, she turned slightly to glance up at him. "My family is so great, don't you think?"

Before Braxton could reply, Jackie shouted impishly, "Oh, look! Kennedy and Braxton are under the mistletoe!"

Startled, Kennedy quickly looked up. Sure enough, right above her head, hanging traitorously from a light fixture, was a small sprig of mistletoe. "I take it back," Kennedy muttered as she wondered how and when it got there. Which one of her meddling siblings would play such a humiliating joke? Her face on fire, she quickly tried to step away, but she looked back in confusion when she felt Braxton's hands catch her shoulders. "Jackie's just teasing us," she informed him.

Smiling, he turned her around to face him. He took her mug from her hands and set it down beside his on a nearby sofa table. "Kennedy," he said, "I'm shocked. You of all people should not balk at such a venerable Christmas tradition." Before she had time to resist, he pulled her tightly into his arms and placed a soft, chaste kiss squarely on her mouth.

Wide-eyed and speechless, Kennedy stared at him in shock, while her family clapped and cheered. Laughing, Braxton released her with a wink and retrieved her mug, pressing it into her hands as if nothing had happened.

When Braxton started talking with her brother-in-law, Kennedy gratefully escaped to the kitchen. Slowly pouring what remained of her hot chocolate down the sink, Kennedy couldn't refrain from placing her fingers to her lips. They were still tingling, and she felt like crying. What was obviously no big deal for Braxton was a life-altering oxymoron for her. The kiss had been brief, but amazingly wonderful, and yet horrible at the same time. She had stupidly fallen for him, and there wasn't a thing she could do about it now. Why had she insisted on him staying for Christmas? She was a masochist and an idiot, and that was all there was to it.

"Hey, pumpkin." Her father startled her from behind, bringing in a tray full of empty hot chocolate mugs. "You okay?"

Pasting a smile on her face she turned around and fibbed. "Yeah, I was just cleaning up a little."

"How about you let me finish up in here. Everyone else has gone off to bed, and I think Braxton is waiting for you in the family room." He winked and placed the tray in the sink.

She reminded herself that she needed to act like nothing had happened. "Okay, thanks, Dad," she said. Reaching up, she kissed him softly on the cheek. "See you in the morning."

Kennedy found Braxton thumbing through a magazine on the couch. She willed her racing heart to calm down a notch. "You'd better get to bed if you want Santa to come," she said nonchalantly.

Glancing up, he smiled. "I've been waiting for you. Where'd you go anyway?" She told him the same thing she'd told her father. Nodding, he stood. "Do you want to go for a walk?"

"Uh . . . sure." Mentally kicking herself for her inability to say no, Kennedy mutely followed him to the coat closet, where he pulled out her coat and helped her put it on. He shrugged into his own jacket, opened the door, and they both headed outside.

After walking in silence for a few minutes, Braxton grinned down at her. "You were right, you know. Your family is great. Thanks for making me stay."

Kennedy smiled at his kind words, wishing she could agree with him. At that moment, she was angry with her traitorous family and sorry for making him stay. "Well, I hope it turns out to be a fun Christmas for you."

They walked a little further in a slightly uncomfortable silence before Kennedy asked tentatively, "Do you think your mom and sisters ever found out about your father's death?"

Braxton was startled by her question. "To be honest, I have no idea. There was a short article in the paper the next day about the CEO of Taylor Homes getting killed in a car accident, but after I tried calling her and got hung up on, I just gave up. My anger got the better of me for a while, and then I realized my attitude wasn't doing anything for me. As time passed, it got easier not to dwell on it, and I just try not to think about them too much."

"That's understandable," Kennedy said quietly.

"But . . . ?" Braxton knew she had something she wanted to say.

"But have you ever thought of giving it another try?"

"No way," Braxton replied quickly, uncomfortable with what he knew Kennedy wanted him to do.

"Time can change people's attitudes sometimes," Kennedy gently reminded him.

"That's what I thought when I tried to call her after his passing." He shook his head at the memory. "It had been five years since the divorce, and the minute she found out who I was, she hung up."

"I know, but maybe you could give it another try," she prodded.

Braxton took a deep breath and replied carefully. "I appreciate what you are trying to do Kennedy, but it won't work. My mother is hard and stubborn, and my sisters have followed her example. And if it's okay with you, I really don't want to talk about it anymore."

Even Kennedy could take a hint eventually. "Okay," she agreed guiltily, feeling like she had ruined his Christmas Eve. Looking up the street, she smiled at the many displays of colored and white Christmas lights. Oh, how she loved Christmas. It was so magical and special. Trying to think of something to lighten the solemn mood she'd produced, Kennedy suddenly had an idea. Grabbing Braxton's arm, she began pulling him forward. "C'mon, I want to show you something."

"What?"

"It's a surprise." She dragged him down a street that ended in a cul-de-sac. Soon they were facing a large home at the end of the street.

Braxton raised an eyebrow. "It's kind of late to be visiting someone, isn't it?"

Rolling her eyes, she ignored his question and towed him to the side of the house where they came across a dark, narrow path. Braxton eyed the path, looking skeptical. It was a dirt trail, sandwiched between two homes with large cinder block fences on either side. The lack of light made it impossible to see beyond twenty feet. "Where exactly are we going?"

"It wouldn't be a surprise if I told you, now would it?" She looked back at him and smiled. "Come on. Trust me."

They carefully made their way through the path, unable to see much of anything. Kennedy kept a firm grasp on his arm, easily leading him along. After about five minutes, they ran into a solid wood door. Braxton could see dim light between the cracks in the panels. There was an old padlock fastened to a large latch. After twisting the dial, Kennedy unlatched the door and led him into what appeared to be a vacant park. Only it wasn't an ordinary park. It was covered with trees, evergreen bushes, and dimly lit pathways. A giant ash tree stood off to the side with an old tire swing hanging from one of its branches. A small stagnant fountain was nestled among plants in one corner. Braxton was transfixed by the serenity and beauty of the place. "Wow," was all he could think to say.

"I know." She smiled at the look on his face. "You should see it in the summer when all of the leaves are on the trees and the flowers are in bloom. After seeing the movie *The Secret Garden*, a family in our neighborhood—they live in the house you saw at the end of the cul-de-sac—decided to create a secret garden of their own. They landscaped this land behind their home and put in the pathway, giving the lock code to all their good friends and neighbors. We used to have such a great time playing here as kids, and then, as I got older, I loved to come here in the evenings when it was usually vacant to think or study. It's a special place for me." She looked off in the distance before adding, "I've never brought anyone here."

"Not even Chris?" he asked.

Kennedy thought for a moment before drawing her eyebrows together and cocking her head to one side. "No, not even Chris."

Braxton was touched. Slowly, he turned her toward him and lifted her chin with his fingers. Staring into her beautiful brown eyes he asked, "Why me?"

"I don't know." Her heart started beating faster, and she felt her breath shorten as she watched him move closer. Caught off guard, Kennedy stood there stupefied as his lips met hers. It was a tender and sweet, slightly drawn out kiss, and once again Kennedy was left overwhelmed, dumfounded, and confused. Did he really just intentionally kiss her without mistletoe and family pressure?

"Mmm . . . twice in one day. I could definitely get used to that," he said quietly, watching her closely.

"What?" she spluttered, for lack of anything better to say.

He laughed, wrapped his arms around her, and pulled her close.

"I mean that I've wanted to do that for a long time, and now that I finally have, I'm addicted already."

"You are?" Kennedy murmured, attempting to digest this wonderful and surprising bit of information.

"Here, I'll demonstrate," he said quietly, bending to kiss her again, much more thoroughly this time.

Kennedy's heart was pounding in her chest and thundering in her ears, as she fervently returned his kiss. Finally pulling back, she stared at him wide-eyed. Could he possibly have genuine feelings for her? If so, her heart soared at the possibility and then immediately plummeted when she remembered Stacey. Here she was, having feelings for someone who evidently shared at least some of those feelings, and yet her roommate was back in Arizona thinking and dreaming about this same guy. She felt like such a jerk. She quickly took a step back. "Oh, man." Kennedy didn't realize she uttered the words out loud.

"Not the desired response, but better than nothing, I suppose," Braxton teased, hoping for a little reassurance.

She finally looked up and surveyed him with a worried expression. "I suppose you don't realize how complicated you just made my life."

"Maybe you should explain it to me." He grabbed her hand and pulled her along beside him as they sauntered down one of the paths.

Kennedy was amazed at how good and comfortable it felt to hold his hand. Not quite knowing where to begin, she said the first thing that popped into her mind. "How do you feel about Stacey?"

"Stacey?" Braxton looked puzzled. "She's like a little sister to me. Is that what you mean?"

"Are you sure you don't feel anything more for her?"

"No, I never have. She's a decade younger than me." Braxton was confused at her line of questioning. What did this have to do with him and Kennedy? She always seemed to bring Stacey's name up at the oddest moments. He glanced down at Kennedy's probing eyes and suddenly had an epiphany. "Oh, no, you're not saying that she—" he broke off, not sure how to word it, but from the nod Kennedy gave him, he knew he understood. "But I've never done anything to make her think . . ." Again, he was at a loss for words.

"Why, I do believe that Braxton Taylor is tongue-tied," Kennedy teased, trying to ease the tension a little.

"Believe me, this is not an uncommon occurrence," he murmured, running his fingers through his hair. "It's just that I feel terrible that Stacey got the wrong idea. She's such a great person, and I love her like a sister, but there is nothing beyond that."

Slowing to a stop, Kennedy turned to face him, looking down at his hand holding hers. "Listen, I don't deny that I've started to have feelings for you. I would venture to guess that most girls who've known you have fallen for you at least a little. I've been trying so hard not to care, mostly because I didn't want to hurt Stacey, and partly because I never thought you could return those feelings. I've come to love her as a sister too, but I don't want some little fling destroying my—our—friendship with her," Kennedy concluded softly, pulling her hand from his as she took another step back from him.

Reacting quickly, Braxton grabbed her by the shoulders to keep her from going anywhere. He caressed her arms as his hands slowly traveled down to grasp her fingers, giving her delightful goose bumps. "Listen, Kennedy, it's been a long time since I've cared about someone, and I can tell you right now that I have never felt this way about anyone before. I hope this doesn't scare you away, but I have to be honest and tell you that I think I'm falling in love with you. I don't want Stacey hurt any more than you do, but unless you tell me to take a hike, I'm not going anywhere."

Kennedy felt as though her heart had stopped beating. Had she heard him right? "You think you love me?" she stuttered. "How? Uh, when? Why?"

"You forgot where and who," he pointed out with a lopsided smile. Pulling her close to him once more, he wrapped his arms around her and held her tightly. "From the day you entered my life with your flat tire and adorably stubborn personality, I haven't been able to get you out of my mind. You are infectious, Kennedy Jackson. You make everyone around you happy. You're sweet, good, talented, intelligent, insanely gorgeous, and amazing. And if you care about me even a little, I am more than willing to risk whatever I have to for you, including Stacey's friendship. This is most assuredly not some 'little fling,' as you put it. Not for me."

Braxton pulled back and saw the tears pooling in Kennedy's eyes. His brows drew together in concern as he studied her beautiful face. "Please don't cry. I realize I've caught you off guard—"

Kennedy placed her hand over his mouth, effectively stopping his dialogue before it could go any further. "I do care about you, Brax, more and more every time I'm with you. I'm only crying because I'm happy." Moving her hand to his cheek, she studied his face as a warm feeling spread through her body. "This feels right to me—you feel right. I would love nothing more than to spend more time with you and get to know you better, but I'm also concerned about Stacey. How about we try not to advertise any relationship that's developing between us, at least not until I find the courage to talk to Stacey. She needs to hear it from me before she finds out on her own."

"Advertise?" he teased. "You're making this sound like a business agreement."

"Right. That way, you'll understand better."

"Not funny." He pulled her into another tight embrace. "Okay," he whispered in her ear. "I agree with your reasoning. But even if this hurts Stacey and possibly ruins our friendship with her, I'm still not going to back off just to ease her mind. Unless, of course, you want me to." He lowered his head for one more kiss. "And I retain the right to kiss you as much as I'd like until we return to Arizona."

Kennedy smiled dreamily up at him. "You mean you aren't leaving the day after Christmas anymore?"

"Not on your life." His lips found hers once again.

�֎ Chapter 12 �֎

"WAKE UP, KENDY! Wake up! It's Cwistmas!" Kennedy awoke with a start to find little Mandy jumping on her bed.

Smiling at her niece's enthusiasm, Kennedy sprang from her bed and grabbed Mandy in a playful hug. "Then let's go get everyone and open presents!"

"Okay, hurry!" Mandy exclaimed as she pulled Kennedy out of her room and down the hall. Noting that Braxton's bedroom door was open, Kennedy peeked inside to find him already gone. She raced Mandy down the stairs where everyone was waiting in the family room.

"Am I the last one awake?" A hurt look of surprise spread across her face as she looked around the room. "I'm never the last one awake."

"Yes, sleepyhead," Kyla commented with a grin. "For a person with your Christmas obsession, I'm shocked."

Kennedy childishly stuck her tongue out at her sister before locating Braxton, who was sporting flannel pajama pants and an old college T-shirt, in a nearby recliner. Deciding to shock her family, she gingerly stepped over to him and plopped onto his lap. She ignored the surprised, pleased look on Braxton's face and the stunned looks from her family and clapped her hands. "Okay, so who's first?"

Five small hands popped into the air, and five tiny voices called out, "Me, me, me!"

Braxton recovered from his surprise, and Kennedy felt his strong arms circle her waist as he pulled her comfortably against him. "Merry Christmas," he whispered in her ear.

"Merry Christmas back." Kennedy squeezed his hand and relaxed against his chest. This was by far the best Christmas she had ever had. As they watched the children open their gifts, Kennedy asked, "How long have you been up?"

"For hours," Braxton teased, but Kennedy's elbow prodded him to tell the truth. "Not long. I think the kids were sent upstairs to wake up you and your parents, but they mistook my room for yours, and, by the time they realized their mistake, I was already awake."

"I'm sorry."

"Don't be," he said. "I had forgotten how fun kids make Christmas."

"They do make it fun," Kennedy replied as she snuggled next to him and watched her family. The children tore into their gifts hungrily while the adults fondly observed. Every now and then Tom would pass a gift out to one of the adults. Kennedy received a cordless power drill from her father with a note attached that read, "Maybe this will help you attract the right guy." Kennedy laughed out loud as she read the note and showed Braxton.

"Wow." Braxton examined the drill. It was a top of the line Bosch. He smiled. "Maybe we should stop seeing each other until you get a few more power tools."

Kennedy glared at him, and her family laughed. Kyla's husband, Mike, grabbed the drill from Braxton. "Man," he said, glancing at his wife, "I knew we got married too young, Kyla!"

Braxton laughed heartily at that comment. He watched as Tom picked up Braxton's gift for Kennedy and passed it along saying, "Here's another one, sweetheart. Maybe it's a screwdriver set."

"Ha, ha," she replied. After glancing at Braxton with half a smile, she removed the tissue paper and peered into the bag. Rolling her eyes, she shook her head at him. "You are so not funny."

He grinned. "You did say you should be a professional."

"I was only kidding!"

"What is it?" Jackie impatiently asked.

Instead of answering, Kennedy lifted two large bristled paint-brushes, a smock, a small can of lavender paint, and a small tarp from the bag.

Laughing, Kennedy's family asked to hear the story, and Braxton gladly complied.

"You got paint all over his new suit?" Jackie was appalled.

"It's not like I meant to," Kennedy defended.

"So, Kenn," Kyla taunted, "when do you think you'll be free to come repaint our house?"

Braxton chuckled as he watched Kennedy banter back and forth with her family. Finally, he interrupted Kennedy by saying, "Are you through making fun of my gift? I can't believe I'm going to tell you this after your ungrateful remarks, but there is still something left in the bag."

Curious, Kennedy lifted up a sheet of crinkled tissue paper, and, sure enough, there was something hidden beneath it. Pulling out a plastic bag with little white flakes in it, Kennedy read the label. "Artificial snow." She raised her eyebrows.

"I thought about getting you a snow machine, but this was easier," Braxton explained. "Now you can have snow on Christmas."

"How sweet!" Smiling, Kennedy opened the bag of snow and sprinkled it over Braxton's head, before kissing him soundly, much to the pleasant surprise of her family. Pulling back, she said, "You know, I would have thought that you'd have given me flour instead."

"I thought about it, but I didn't want to fight with you over who got to clean it up."

Standing, Olivia interrupted everyone by saying, "Who's going to help me with breakfast?"

"Wait!" Kennedy exclaimed, grinning mischievously at Braxton. "There's still one more gift." Jumping off his lap, she ran over to the tree, reached her hand behind it, and pulled out a small gift, wrapped in shiny gold paper with a dark green ribbon. Handing it to Braxton, she said, "Merry Christmas, Brax."

Tearing the wrapping paper off quickly, he pulled out a book and read aloud, "*How to Meet People and Make Friends.*" Rolling his eyes, Braxton tossed the book back at Kennedy.

Kennedy caught the book neatly before it hit her in the ribs. "You're welcome," she said. "I'll help you, Mom," she offered.

"Good," her mother replied as Kennedy followed her into the kitchen. "Then you can explain the meaning behind that book."

Not long after Olivia and Kennedy began breakfast preparations,

Jackie and Kyla burst through the door. Kyla was the first to talk. "Okay, so the boys have gone off to play basketball."

Jackie giggled. "We knew that mistletoe would do the trick!"

"Oh, you two turkeys!" Kennedy accused. "If I weren't so happy at the moment, I'd skin you both alive and cook you for dinner!"

"If only you could cook," Jackie joked.

"That's it," Kennedy said. "I am so telling Kevin about Raoul." Kennedy said, referring to the guy Jackie had kissed while she'd been dating Kevin.

"Don't you dare," Jackie threatened as she grabbed a spatula and started for her sister.

Cracking an egg, Kennedy retorted with a grin. "Personally, I'd rather be hit with a spatula than pelted with raw eggs."

"Kennedy!" Kyla exclaimed. "Will you please stop taunting Jackie and tell us what happened last night!"

"All right!" Kennedy laughed. "To be honest, I have no idea. One minute I'm thinking we're good friends, and the next he shows up here and informs me that he's in love with me."

Both Jackie and Kyla squealed with delight. Olivia smiled warmly and studied her daughter. "How do you feel about him?"

Both sisters watched Kennedy, waiting for her to answer. She answered only with a large smile.

"In comparison to Chris?" her mother questioned.

"He's helped me get over Chris," offered Kennedy. "But don't worry, Mom. I've learned my lesson. I know that I have a lot of praying to do."

Olivia listened while Jackie and Kyla continued to pester Kennedy with questions, wanting to know all the details of their budding relationship.

Later that evening, after everyone had gone to bed, Kennedy lay on the couch with her head on Braxton's lap as he combed through her hair with his fingers. Closing her eyes, she thought about the events of the past couple of months. Granted, she had definitely not seen this relationship coming, but now that it had, she couldn't imagine her life without Braxton. It felt so right to be with him. But wasn't that how she had felt with Chris at first too? The thought made her confused and scared. What if Braxton wasn't right for her either? What if things ended the same way they had with Chris? She didn't think she could go through all of that again, and yet she knew that she couldn't turn back now. That meant putting her faith and trust in God once again.

"What are you thinking about?" Braxton looked down at her tenderly as he twisted her hair around his finger.

"I really don't think you want to know." Kennedy smiled up at him.

"Try me."

"I was thinking that I'm scared." She said the words quietly, as if afraid to say them. "What if I'm headed in the wrong direction again? I'm afraid that Heavenly Father will want to take you away from me too."

He smiled. "Have you ever considered the possibility that the reason you needed to break things off with Chris and move to Arizona was to meet and fall for me?"

Not knowing what to say, she merely smiled. "Aren't you cocky?"

Chuckling, Braxton sat her up and promptly gathered her in his arms. "Well, I guarantee that He wants you to marry someone sometime."

"What are you saying, Braxton?" Kennedy teased, trying to slow her heartbeat and breathing.

"Would it scare you if I told you that I would marry you tomorrow if you'd let me?"

"Slightly, yes." Kennedy searched Braxton's face, as she pulled away from him. "You can't be serious. You really don't even know me that well."

"You're right. I don't know what your favorite color is, though my money is on green since it shows up so much in your decorating. I don't know what grades you got in high school math, but I'll bet my newly painted suit that they were probably A's. And I don't know what your favorite movie is, but I would venture it falls under the romantic comedy genre—something like *Pride and Prejudice*." He grabbed a hold of her trembling hands and held them securely within his grasp before he continued, "But I do know that you are extremely talented, genuinely kind, breathtakingly beautiful, and annoyingly witty. I also know that you are courageous, strong-willed, intelligent, and most important—close to the Lord. And seeing you with your family these past couple of days has shown me another wonderful side to you." Braxton lifted his hand to her cheek and caressed it lightly. "Kennedy, I adore you. You make me want to be a better person, and I love how I feel when I'm with you. I've prayed about it, and I have no doubt that you're someone the Lord is okay with me spending the eternities with."

Kennedy quickly wiped at the tears threatening to run down her face. Her head was reeling, and she had no idea what to say. Thankfully, she didn't have to say anything, because he continued talking.

"Listen, Kenn, I know I've thrown a lot at you in the last forty-eight hours, and I know you have a lot to think and pray about. I'm not asking for any answers or promises from you until you are ready to give them. I just wanted you to know how I am feeling."

Kennedy gave up wiping at the tears and let them spill down her cheeks. "You're pretty amazing yourself, you know." Kennedy smiled. "I think I'm falling in love with you too. How could I not? But you're right—I do need time to figure some things out."

He nodded his understanding as he tightened his arms around her once again. Glancing around the room, he spied the ball the guys had used earlier that day to play basketball. "Hey, Kenn," he said, raising his eyebrows in challenge, "how about a quick game of Horse before bed?"

She pulled away with a baffled expression on her face. Was he serious?

"I'm serious." Evidently reading minds was one of his talents as well. "I noticed that secret park of yours has a small basketball court on one side. Are you game?"

Her eyes flew to the clock on the wall. "But it's one o'clock in the morning, and it's chilly tonight!"

"I think I can manage to keep you warm." He winked suggestively, and pulled her up into his arms, giving her a lingering kiss.

Kennedy smiled up at him. "You're on, my friend. But I have to warn you—I never lose at Horse."

"Obviously, you've never played me." He grabbed the ball and opened the door for her, whispering in her ear as she walked past. "First one there gets the ball to start with."

Before she had a chance to react, he jogged past her. "Cheater!" she called after him as she raced to catch up.

❊

Kennedy had no desire to return to Tempe and reality. The couple of weeks she had spent with her family and Braxton had been utter bliss. He had become part of her family—part of her life. Her family adored him, and Kennedy knew she was already hopelessly in love with him. Wanting the week after Christmas to go on forever, Kennedy woke up completely depressed the morning they had to leave for Phoenix. She would grudgingly give up hot chocolate for a year not to have to face Stacey or Shauna ever again.

The only plus was that Braxton, who had caravanned behind her the entire way, would be there. And so it was with trepidation that she waved good-bye to Braxton's Silverado and pulled into her apartment complex's parking lot. He had offered to go with her when she talked to Stacey, but Kennedy knew it would only make it worse. Stacey would be mortified if she knew Braxton had learned of her feelings for him.

Staring through the darkness up at her apartment door with foreboding, Kennedy took a deep breath and pulled her keys from the ignition. "Well, here goes nothing," she muttered.

She grabbed her duffel bag from the backseat and slowly headed up the walkway, racking her brain for the kindest way to break Stacey's heart. The task would be impossible—only weeks before Kennedy had stupidly informed her roommate that Braxton liked Stacey. Kennedy recalled the excited look on Stacey's face after their conversation, and she knew that she'd given Stacey hope. Now, here she was, only weeks later, planning to massacre that hope as well as any sort of friendship she had made with Stacey.

Kennedy felt horrible. Secretly, she had been praying that Stacey would meet someone during the break and fall madly in love by the time Kennedy returned, but she had a feeling that her prayers had not been answered.

As she approached her apartment, Kennedy was stunned to hear a heated argument coming from their living room window. She took a few more steps toward the voices, until she was within hearing range and dropped to the steps to listen. The voices belonged to Stacey and Becca. *How odd*, thought Kennedy, *they never fight.*

"Well, it's my life, isn't it?" Becca shouted. "If I want to get baptized, I will."

"You are an idiot, Becca." Stacey spit the words. "You heard Kennedy talk about her church. You're not just signing up to go to a service once a week for a few hours. You are signing up for an entire lifestyle change. Just because you think you're in love with Jason doesn't mean you should give up your life and go running to join his church. If I were that weak-willed, I'd have joined the church a long time ago. But I refuse to change my belief system, even for B. J."

"Stacey, have you even been listening to me? I'm joining because I believe, not just so I can marry Jason. I started taking those missionary discussions again with him, and I felt something. So I read their Book of Mormon and felt something more. And every discussion, I felt more and more until I suddenly realized that I wanted to be baptized more than anything, because I know it's true. Oh, Stace, how could you not feel it too?"

"Oh please, Becca. That wonderful feeling is just you being in love with Jason, not some spiritual manifestation. Otherwise, why didn't you feel that way when you sat in on some of the discussions with me?"

"Because I didn't really pay attention then."

"Well, maybe you should start taking Jason to all your classes with you. Perhaps he'll inspire your grades to improve."

"You know, it's no use talking to you while you are in this mood."

"What mood?" Stacey practically shrieked.

"The 'Braxton doesn't like me' mood," Becca screamed back. "Why do you keep doing that to yourself? Everyone knows he likes you, so stop with the pity party and grow up."

Before Kennedy realized what was happening, the door flung open, and Becca charged out, slamming it behind her in a huff. Kennedy jumped up and watched guiltily. Somewhere in the apartment, another door slammed. Stacey must have shut herself in her room.

"Uh, I didn't mean to eavesdrop," Kennedy explained hesitantly.

"How could you not?" Becca gestured toward the open window. "I'm sure the entire complex inadvertently overheard our conversation. And if I were you, I probably wouldn't go in there for awhile."

"Yeah, got that," Kennedy quipped. "Where are you going?"

"Well, Jason is expecting me to come over, but I'm afraid that my current mood might make him want to move out of the state. So I was planning to call and make up an excuse."

"Want some company?" offered Kennedy.

"Sure, why not?" Becca replied glumly. "If our fight doesn't make you want to move to another country."

No, just to another apartment, Kennedy thought as the two strode back to her car. Now how was she ever going to talk to Stacey?

After Becca quickly phoned Jason with some excuse about not going over, the two rode in silence for some time. Finally, Kennedy asked, "Was there anywhere in particular you wanted to go?"

"You mentioned once that you like to go to your temple when you need to think," Becca suggested hesitantly.

Without a word, Kennedy made a U-turn and headed in the direction of the temple. She wanted so badly to talk to Becca about her sudden decision to be baptized, but Kennedy was afraid to bring up the subject. It was probably best to leave Becca to her own thoughts at the moment.

They arrived at the temple, and Kennedy led Becca to a courtyard between the temple and the visitor's center. They found a bench in a fairly secluded area and made themselves comfortable.

After a few minutes of silence, Becca commented quietly, "How could she think I'd make such a life-changing decision just for a guy? Granted, I am crazy about Jason, but I wouldn't join a church just to marry him. I thought Stacey knew me better than that."

Kennedy wasn't sure whether Becca was speaking rhetorically or if she wanted an answer, so she stayed quiet and continued to listen.

"I believe, Kennedy." A small tear crept down Becca's cheek. "And I don't think it's love talking. I felt something every time I would listen to those missionaries—something that brought me peace and joy and gave me goose bumps. If Jason told me tomorrow that he didn't want to see me anymore, I would still be baptized. Granted, I'd be completely heartbroken and choose another ward to attend," Becca smiled wryly, "but I'd still get baptized." She glanced at Kennedy and pleaded, "You believe me, don't you?"

"Of course I do, Becca. I've felt the Holy Ghost throughout my life, so I know what you're talking about. I am so happy and excited for you," Kennedy responded with a smile as she put an arm around Becca. "Don't worry about Stacey. I'm sure she'll come around eventually."

"Oh, I don't think she's really mad at me. She seems to have a crazy idea that B. J. likes you instead of her, so she just took that hurt out on me." Becca sniffled, wiping the tears from her eyes with her shirtsleeve. "What she said definitely upset me, but I know she'll apologize after she's cooled off a little. I just wish B. J. would get around to dating her, instead of waiting for her to join the church. She's going to go crazy otherwise."

Kennedy suddenly developed an uncomfortable feeling in the pit in her stomach. Dropping her arm, she leaned forward and placed her face in her hands. Should she talk to Becca before she talked to Stacey? Would Becca hate her too? Taking a chance, Kennedy decided to come clean. "Becca," she began slowly. "Umm, I think you may be wrong about Braxton."

"What do you mean?"

"I mean, I don't think he's waiting for her to join the church so he can date her." Kennedy cast Becca a worried glance. "In fact, I know he's not."

"How do you know that?" Becca asked carefully.

"Because he told me." Kennedy's fingers twisted together nervously.

"Oh, dear," Becca said sadly. "How in the world did you guys get on that topic?"

Well, it's now or never, Kennedy thought. Taking a deep breath, she peered down at her feet. "I decided to ask him about it after he surprised me when he showed up at my house over Christmas and kissed me."

"He did what?" Becca eyes widened to twice their size. "And you didn't know he was coming?"

"I swear I had no idea," Kennedy confessed painfully. "I don't deny that I was developing some feelings for him, but I never would have done anything about them because of Stacey. Besides, I thought he only cared about me as a friend—nothing more."

"So you guys are dating now?" Becca questioned, her eyes still wide with shock.

Kennedy nodded glumly.

"Is it serious?"

Kennedy felt sick. "He told me he loves me." Love was supposed to be fun and exciting. It shouldn't cause so much trouble.

"Oh, man." Becca shook her head in disbelief. "And I thought I had problems."

"I told Braxton I wanted to talk to Stacey before anything else happened between us, and he made me promise I'd do it tonight, as soon as I got home. But there is no way I can talk to her now."

"What are you going to tell her then? And when?"

"I have no idea," Kennedy confessed. "A month ago, I was assuring her of Braxton's regard for her, and now here I am—dating him myself. I feel like such a hypocrite!"

"Well, no offense, but you are one," Becca pointed out and then began to laugh. "This really is funny in a morbid sort of way."

Kennedy glared at Becca. "It is most definitely not funny."

Sobering, Becca murmured contritely, "Sorry. It's just that I suddenly felt a little better knowing that you have bigger problems with Stacey than I do."

"Gee, thanks," Kennedy replied sarcastically. "Would you like me to get hit by a car? That ought to make you feel even better."

"Don't be ridiculous. Of course it wouldn't make me feel better. Then I'd have to call an ambulance and go to the hospital with you."

"I could really hit *you* right now."

"Go ahead. It might make you feel better," Becca teased. "Seriously though, what are you going to say to Stace?"

"Do you have any ideas?"

"Sorry, I'm fresh out."

"But you know her better than I do."

"I know—which is why I want you to warn me before you talk to her, so I can be gone on a long vacation."

"And to think, I thought you would actually be of some help." Kennedy closed her eyes in exasperation.

"Well, I do think you should do as B. J. suggested and tell her right away," Becca stated flatly. Kennedy's raised her eyebrows. "And not just because it will redirect her from me, but because she's going to be even more upset if she finds out you kept it from her."

"I know," Kennedy said, sighing. "I just wish there was some way to tell her without making her hate me."

"That might be asking the impossible," replied Becca honestly.

❋ Chapter 13 ❋

S TACEY WAS FURIOUS. She felt like her world was collapsing in around her, and she couldn't do anything about it. Regardless of what Becca said, she knew that B. J. cared more for Kennedy than everyone seemed to think. Her only hope was that Kennedy didn't like B. J. in return. But how could she not? He was perfect. And now Becca was joining the Mormon Church. Stacey felt betrayed somehow. Like her best friend was going to change and things would never be the same.

Suddenly she had to get out. The apartment emanated loneliness, and Stacey couldn't bear it any longer. It was as if the place typified what her future held for her. In her urgency to leave the claustrophobia behind, she grabbed her keys and rushed to her car. Her thoughts consumed her as she drove through the city streets, headed for nowhere in particular.

She blamed Kennedy for all this. If only she had never moved to Arizona. Then B. J. would still be Stacey's, and Becca would never have met Jason. Everything would have been perfect. Instead, though, everything was exactly the opposite—completely messed up.

Slowly, she became aware of her surroundings. Without realizing it, she had driven straight to B. J.'s street. How many times had she driven here before just to be near something of his, wishing he would finally see her as more than a sister. But now that was not to be. Instead of anger, all Stacey felt was a deep painful emptiness. Knowing B. J. was most likely still on his business trip in New Mexico, Stacey felt no qualms about parking directly in front of his house. She turned off her ignition, placed her head on the steering wheel, and finally gave way to her emotions, letting the tears fall. She was so caught up in her own misery that she failed to see B. J. come out his front door, a garbage bag in hand.

Braxton recognized Stacey's bright red Mazda Miata immediately. Realizing she hadn't seen him, he quickly crossed over to the trash, threw in the garbage bag, and headed back toward her car. As he approached, he saw that she was sobbing uncontrollably. Kennedy must have already talked to her, but he had no idea why Stacey had come to his house. And why didn't she knock on the door? He was confused and unsure of what to do.

Watching Stacey cry, his heart went out to her. She was such a good friend, and he hated the fact that his relationship with Kennedy would most likely ruin that friendship—at least until Stacey fell in love with someone else. But the fact was that he loved Kennedy, and it was better for Stacey to know that he would never care about her as more than a friend. She needed to move on.

Not knowing what else to do, but wanting to offer whatever comfort he could, Braxton knocked quietly on her window until he got her attention.

Stacey jumped at the sudden noise. Glancing out her window, she was mortified to see Braxton standing there. How was she going to explain her distraught appearance, let alone her presence at his house?

She quickly dried her eyes and unrolled the window, wanting desperately to flee the situation. But she'd have to face him sooner or later, so she might as well get it over with.

"Hey, you okay, Stace?" The concern was evident on his face.

"Yeah, I'm fine, just completely embarrassed." Stacey looked at the steering wheel self-consciously.

"I know it's late, but do you want to come in for a minute and talk?" he offered.

Stacey nodded and followed him inside. He led her to the recliner in the family room and asked if she'd like a drink or something to eat. She politely declined and continued to wipe at her eyes and look miserable.

"I'm sorry to show up like this, B. J. I just got into a terrible fight, and I didn't know where else to go."

He sat down on the sofa beside her. "I'm so sorry. I assume you're referring to Kennedy."

Stacey looked at him sharply. "You mean Becca, don't you? Kennedy isn't even back yet."

"She's not?" He was confused. Why would she have fought with Becca?

"No. She's supposed to be back some time tonight but as of fifteen minutes ago, she still wasn't home."

Now he was completely puzzled. It had been nearly an hour since he waved good-bye and watched Kennedy drive into her parking lot. Suddenly he began to worry. What if something had happened to her? He knew he should have followed her into the parking lot and waited until she was safely inside. Did she have to go somewhere? No. When they stopped for dinner, she mentioned how she couldn't wait to get home to take a long, hot shower and get to sleep. She had teased Braxton that he kept her up way too late. She had even mentioned that grocery shopping would have to wait until the next day. Where could she be? The thought made him nervous.

Stacey was still speaking, ". . . I didn't mean to get so mad at her. I just wanted Becca to think about her decision before she charged recklessly ahead like she always does about so many things. But you know Becca—"

"I'm sorry to interrupt, Stacey, but are you sure Kennedy wasn't back yet?"

Looking hurt and a little stunned, Stacey reaffirmed. "I'm positive. There was only Becca and me at the apartment. But she could be home by now if you want to call and see." Braxton was being callous. Instead of being the good listener he usually was, all he cared about was whether Kennedy was home or not. *He probably can't wait to see her again*, Stacey thought bitterly. Stacey stood up. "I can see you're preoccupied with other things," she said miserably, "so I'll be on my way now."

Realizing that Stacey had misunderstood him, Braxton tried to explain. "No, it's not that." He saw no other way around it but to tell her the truth. "It's just that I followed Kennedy back from New Mexico and saw her drive into the parking lot a good hour ago." Braxton rubbed his head, wondering what to do.

"What?" Stacey questioned. "Why were you following her home?"

"Hold on." Braxton grabbed his phone and quickly dialed Kennedy's cell number. *Please answer, please answer,* he repeated to himself as the phone went directly to her voice mail. She must have turned off her phone. Suddenly he felt an urgency to go to Kennedy's apartment and find out what had happened to her. Grabbing Stacey's arm, he dragged her toward his garage door. "I'll explain in the car. Right now we need to go find Kennedy and make sure she's okay."

Pulling away from his grasp, Stacey glared at him. "I've got to be somewhere. Why don't you go check on her and I'll see you later?"

Rolling his eyes in frustration, Braxton tried to remain calm. "After I make sure Kennedy is all right, I want to finish talking to you, so please come with me."

"Fine," Stacey said woodenly, following him to the truck.

The two drove in an uncomfortable silence as B. J. raced toward the apartment building. Ten minutes later, he plowed over the speed bumps and into the nearest parking space. Immediately, he spotted her car. Praying that Kennedy had just forgotten about an errand she needed to run, and that she was now safely back in the apartment, Braxton recklessly jumped out, forgetting Stacey was right behind him. He bounded up the stairs two at a time and burst through the front door. He stopped abruptly, when he saw Kennedy and Becca, calmly sipping hot chocolate and talking. Stacey followed at a more sedate pace, rolling her eyes when she saw both her roommates. Kennedy and Becca stared at them nonplussed.

Braxton was the first to speak. "Oh, Kenn, thank goodness you're okay," he explained breathlessly, kicking the door shut with his foot.

Kennedy looked hesitantly from Braxton to Stacey, wondering why they were together and whether he had gone insane. "And why wouldn't I be okay?"

"Where have you been for the past hour?"

Rather than answer his question, she simply stared at him with her forehead wrinkled and her eyebrow raised, as if wondering why he was asking. She wasn't about to say that she'd gone for a drive with Becca while Stacey was listening.

Braxton realized that it probably looked a little odd that he had come barging in with Stacey, insisting that he know her whereabouts. Finding the entire situation humorous, he gave a low chuckle as he collapsed on the armchair. "Sorry, that came out wrong. Stacey just showed up at my house fifteen minutes ago and told me she just left the apartment and you hadn't come home yet. Naturally, I was a little worried."

"A little worried?" Becca asked with raised eyebrows.

Braxton simply shrugged as if everything had been explained. He didn't make the mistake of asking Kennedy where she had gone again, even though he was curious.

Suddenly, the atmosphere in the room changed from mild chaos to an uncomfortable silence. Becca was the first to flee the scene. "Well, it's getting late, and I have an early class tomorrow, so good night all!" She jumped up and headed down the hall.

Not wanting to be in the same room with Becca or Kennedy, Stacey just stood there, wondering what to do.

Finally, Kennedy shot Braxton a meaningful look, as if to say, "Now is not the best time for you to be here," before turning to Stacey. "Hey, Stace, before you go to bed, I was wondering if I could talk to you for a minute."

Braxton knew he had left things unfinished with Stacey. He realized with trepidation that he had better talk to her about Kennedy while he was at it. So rather than make his excuses to leave, he mustered up his courage. "Hey, I'm sure whatever Kennedy has to say to you can wait," he told Stacey. "She looks tired. How about you come out for a bowl of ice cream with me, and then we'll go pick up your car?"

Stacey hesitated. She didn't want to talk to anyone at the moment, but since B. J. seemed to be the lesser of the three evils, she grudgingly agreed. Opening the door, she walked back outside and started down the stairs ahead of B. J.

Braxton watched Stacey leave, before turning back to catch Kennedy's eye. Her expression was puzzled, and yet grateful at the same time. She mouthed the words, "I love you," and blew him a kiss.

Mustering a smile, he nodded as if to say, "You'd better," and closed the door behind him. Walking after Stacey, he mentally berated himself as he wondered how he had gotten into this situation. Ever since he'd met Kennedy, his organized, comfortable life had become a serious of misadventures, mixed with mayhem. Now, he was in the worst fix yet. He hated confrontation with women, especially where hurt feelings were involved. Knowing he had no one to blame but himself, he followed in Stacey's wake, muttering under his breath, "Kennedy owes me big time for this."

✳ ✿ ✳

Twenty minutes later, Braxton and Stacey were sitting in a secluded booth at a nearby ice cream parlor, spooning frozen yogurt into their mouths.

Deciding to break the silence, he asked casually, "What did you and Becca argue about anyway?"

Stacey watched him in silence, debating whether or not she was ready to forgive him for being so insensitive. Knowing she couldn't stay mad at him forever, she finally decided to let him off the hook. "Remember Jason? That guy she met at your stake party? Well, Becca thinks she in love with him, so she's planning to join your church."

Braxton was surprised. "You mean, she's getting baptized?"

"Yeah."

"And you don't think it's for the right reasons?"

"Well, Becca assured me that she would get baptized even if things didn't work out with Jason, but I really don't think she would."

"Why not?"

"Because it has all happened too quickly. Becca has always been too reckless. I told her she needed to give her decision some more thought, and she practically told me that I was crazy for thinking that." Stacey looked earnestly at Braxton. "Don't you think two weeks is way too soon to make a life-changing decision?"

"Well, I think it all depends," he replied thoughtfully. "I've seen people take years before they gain a testimony of the gospel, and others, only a matter of days. And some, never. Everyone is different."

Stacey rolled her eyes. "I guess I should have known that you'd take her side. I'm sure you are thrilled to hear she wants to be baptized. Another person to check off your list."

"Ouch," Braxton stated with a frown. "That's not how it is at all, Stacey. I know the joy and peace the gospel brings to people. I've seen it in their eyes, and I've seen it change lives. If that's the case with Becca, you're right—I'm thrilled. But I don't want her, or you, for that matter, to ever get baptized without gaining a testimony first. I don't have some stupid quota I'm trying to fill, Stace. That's not how it works."

Stacey sighed. "I know, and I'm sorry. I'm just worried about Becca."

"Well, that's understandable, considering you are her best friend." Braxton gave a small smile. "But I hope you know that if Becca does join the church and you don't, you guys will still be best friends, and you can still live next door to each other like you planned."

Stacey nodded. "I guess I really should go and apologize to her, huh?"

Braxton smiled. He had finished his frozen yogurt and noticed Stacey was practically done with hers, but he still needed to talk to her about Kennedy. Not quite knowing where to start, he said lamely, "Hey, there's something else I wanted to talk to you about."

"What?" Stacey inquired, more than happy to remain in the ice cream parlor with B. J.

"Uh, it's about Kennedy."

Stacey's heart sank at the mere mention of her roommate's name. Why couldn't she have one conversation with B. J. without the mention of Kennedy? "What about her?"

"Well . . . I just wanted you to know that Kennedy and I are dating," he said lamely, not knowing what else to say.

Stacey's night had actually gotten worse, if that was possible. She felt as though her entire life was ruined. Bitterness and resentment filled her thoughts as she thought of Kennedy and B. J.—her B. J.—together. How could Kennedy do this to her, especially after assuring Stacey that this would not happen? Stacey felt betrayed, but she tried her best not to show it. Camouflaging her inner turmoil, she pasted a smile on her face and said, "That's great. I'm really happy for you guys."

"Really?" Braxton asked. "You sure you're okay with it?"

"Yeah," Stacey returned. "Why wouldn't I be?"

"No reason, I just wanted you to know." Braxton knew Stacey was lying, and yet he had no idea what to say. Nothing he could think to say would make her feel any better, so he just decided to play along. "Well, thanks for coming out for ice cream with me."

Stacey was trying hard to disguise her hurt and blink back her tears. Not trusting her voice, she merely nodded at him and then reached for her purse, letting him know she was ready to go.

✳ ✿ ✳

As Kennedy knelt to say her prayers the following morning, she felt greedy, like she was asking for much more then she deserved. She asked for Stacey's understanding and prayed that they could eventually be friends again. She prayed for a better attitude at work, particularly with regard to Shauna. But mostly, she pleaded with her Father in Heaven about Braxton, wanting desperately to know that he was someone she could happily spend the rest of her life with.

Wandering into the kitchen, Kennedy grabbed a box of cereal from the top of the refrigerator, poured herself a bowl, and sat down to eat, worry creasing her brow. Her thoughts were disturbed by Stacey's entrance. It didn't take a high school diploma to notice the red around Stacey's eyes. She had been crying—probably most of the night—and Kennedy had no way to ease the pain.

"Hey, Stace, I—"

"Don't." Stacey cut her off quickly as she grabbed a banana and fled the room.

Stacey weighed on Kennedy's mind as she rushed off to work, dreading the reality of facing Shauna once again. Minutes later, she found herself caught in a rush-hour traffic jam on the freeway. Impatiently drumming her fingers on the steering wheel, she glanced at her watch, dismayed to see that she would be late—one more thing for Shauna to get upset about. Just then her cell phone rang.

She grabbed the phone from her purse. "Hello?"

"Hey, beautiful." Braxton's voice sent chills through her body.

"Hey back," she replied with a smile. "What are you up to?"

"Just calling to make sure you were planning to turn in your notice today, so you can work for me."

"Wouldn't that be nice."

"Kennedy, you think I'm joking, but I'm not. Caroline whole-heartedly agrees, I might add."

Kennedy was taken back by his frankness but pleased at the offer. If only she could. "Braxton, I did think you were joking, but, however tempting that is, I gave my word that I'd stay with Interior Essentials for at least a year. So until the middle of August, I'm stuck."

"Are you serious?" Braxton didn't bother to hide his frustration.

"I'm afraid so," Kennedy replied dismally. "So that means that I get to go back to work today as a glorified secretary. Wish me luck."

"Well, I suppose we can talk about this later," he responded. "The other thing I was calling about was to see if you'd care to join me for dinner tonight—oh, and to see if you wouldn't mind clearing your schedule for me tomorrow evening also."

"Both sound wonderful. I don't have any plans." Kennedy smiled. Her day suddenly seemed brighter.

"Great. I'll pick you up at six-thirty tonight, then." The line went dead, and Kennedy chuckled to herself as she recalled Braxton's business-like way of asking her out. It sounded more like a request for a work meeting than for a dinner date. No wonder she hadn't realized he was interested in her before he flat-out told her.

Kennedy's good mood lasted until she arrived at the office and hurried up to her desk. Shauna was waiting for her, leaning against Kennedy's desk, rapidly tapping her foot on the carpeted floor.

"You're late," Shauna stated curtly.

Kennedy knew she should have expected this. "Sorry, I got stuck in traffic," Kennedy replied readily. "Was there something you needed?"

"Yes," Shauna affirmed coolly. "You see, I too took some time off for the holidays, though not nearly as much as you did, and while I was gone I had my phone redirected to your answering machine. I need my messages."

Kennedy couldn't believe Shauna's pettiness. What was her problem? Trying to control her rising temper, she failed miserably.

"Well, if it's any consolation, Suzi, Katie, and I almost had to cut our break short because of some miscommunications with the painter and the furniture store, but thankfully Braxton bailed us out, and we were able to complete our project and return home as planned." Kennedy watched Shauna's jaw harden at this thinly veiled diatribe. "You wouldn't know anything about that, would you?" Kennedy asked, watching Shauna's eyes narrow in fury.

"I would just work on my communication and organization skills if I were you." Shauna's voice was like steel.

Kennedy smiled sweetly and ignored Shauna's comment, realizing that confronting her supervisor was a futile way to spend her time and energy. Instead she merely said, "I'm afraid I haven't had a chance to check the messages yet, but as soon as I do, you will be the first to know."

"Please be quick about it." Shauna turned abruptly and retreated down the hall to her office.

Kennedy rolled her eyes and purposely took her time getting situated. She even went to the break room to get a cup of water first and ran into Suzi.

"Hey, Kenn!" Suzi exclaimed. "How was your holiday?"

"So fun," Kennedy said warmly. She was so grateful to see Suzi's cheerful face. "How about yours?"

"It was really nice, but I was excited to come back to work. Betty acquired a contract for a new ritzy hotel going up in Phoenix. She was so pleased with the work we did for Taylor Homes that she's given me a lot of responsibility with this new job." Betty was Suzi's supervisor.

"I'm so happy for you." Kennedy was excited for her friend. Suzi was extremely talented and such a hard worker that she deserved it, but Kennedy couldn't help but feel a prick of jealousy. If only Shauna were as kind.

"Well, I better run," Suzi said. "But let's do lunch sometime soon, okay?"

"I'll plan on it." Kennedy decided she had stalled long enough, so she quickly filled her mug up with cold water and returned to her desk. Picking up the phone, she hit the message button and groaned when she heard the computerized voice recount, "You have twenty-nine new messages." Dinner could not come soon enough.

❀ Chapter 14 ❀

T HE FOLLOWING WEEKS passed slowly for Kennedy. She had to
refrain from giving her notice to Shauna several times, but her
desire to hold true to her word kept her from giving up completely.
That, and a familiar feeling that she was doing the right thing by
staying. She had learned many times in her life that the Lord knew
more than she did, and if she just trusted Him and followed the
quiet promptings, things would work out for the best. So she continued to putter along, praying for patience.

One particular morning in early February, she arrived at work
and checked her voicemail only to find several messages for Shauna.
Exasperated, she jotted down the names and numbers, took a deep
breath, and headed into Shauna's office, determined not to loose
her cool. Instead of fighting for composure, though, Kennedy found
herself struggling to keep her jaw from plummeting to the floor.
Shauna's office was empty. Except for the furniture, there were no
pictures on the walls, no well-groomed plants on her bookshelf, no
clutter on her desk, and most significantly—no Shauna. Was she
switching offices? Did she get a promotion? Kennedy was mysti-
fied.

She was even more baffled minutes later when the administra-
tive assistant to the CEO came by and told Kennedy that her boss
would like to see her in his office promptly. Not knowing what to
say, Kennedy followed the secretary until she was shown into a spacious office. Interior Essentials was a fairly large corporation, and,
aside from being briefly introduced to Mr. Caymen months before,
Kennedy had had no other interaction with the president.

There was a reason James Caymen was not in a helping profession. His manner would have scared away Ebenezer Scrooge. He offered no welcoming smile or salutation. He only studied Kennedy for a moment before gesturing to an armchair near his desk. Quietly, Kennedy seated herself, hoping he was going to provide answers regarding Shauna's absence.

He wasted no time with casualties. "As you've probably surmised, Shauna is no longer with our company. Since it was a rather abrupt departure, we are left in somewhat of a bind." Once again, his eyes regarded Kennedy as he leaned back with a slight frown creasing his stern face. "We are hoping to fill her position soon, but until then I need you to help us out. Basically, all you'll need to do is keep the office running. Do you think you can manage that?"

"It shouldn't be a problem."

"Good," he stated dismissively. "We'll let you know when a replacement has been found."

"Uh, Mr. Caymen . . ." Kennedy couldn't stop herself. "Do you know why—"

"I make it a point not to participate in any inter-office gossip, especially where employees are concerned."

Having been rebuffed, Kennedy retreated from his office even more bewildered than before. Why did Shauna leave? Where did she go? Kennedy had no qualms about holding down the office. That's all she'd been doing the past month anyway. Kennedy shook her head and walked back to her desk, resolving to bury her curiosity and get to work. She realized she might never receive any answers to her questions.

"Hey!" Suzi and Katie startled Kennedy at her desk later that afternoon. "What happened with Shauna? I heard she quit, but no one seems to know the reason."

"Well, you can add me to your list," Kennedy replied. "I have no idea either."

"Strange," mused Katie. "You'd think she'd have at least told you."

"We weren't exactly the best of friends," Kennedy said grimly.

"Well, if you hear anything, let us know."

"Same goes for you."

They nodded as they retreated back to their desks.

✳ ✿ ✳

"Shauna quit," Kennedy announced to Braxton that night. He had made her dinner at his house, teasing her about coming over early so he could give her a cooking lesson.

"Seriously?" Braxton asked as he cut through his steak, grinning at the news. "That's awesome!"

"Yeah, it is," Kennedy murmured thoughtfully as she played with the asparagus on her plate.

"Don't tell me you aren't glad." He stared at her across the table.

"No. I mean, I am." She wrinkled her brow. "It just all happened so suddenly, and I can't keep myself from wondering why she left and where she went."

"Good riddance, in my opinion," he said candidly.

"She was a top designer at Interior Essentials, probably the most prestigious interior design firm in the western United States, and she just up and leaves? Are you not just a little curious?"

"Not really," he said honestly, taking a bite of his baked potato. "I'm just happy you don't have to put up with her anymore."

"Well, it's driving me crazy." Kennedy picked up her cup and swirled her water around. "I really don't care much for Shauna, but I do hope she's okay."

Smiling, Braxton reached across the table and took her hand. "You can't solve everyone's problems."

"I know, I know. I just haven't been able to get my mind off her all day."

"Well, maybe I can help with that." He let go of her hand and returned his attention to his dinner.

Kennedy waited for him to say more and when he didn't, she put her fork down and said, "You can't just make a comment like that and leave me hanging."

"If you'd quit playing with your dinner and actually eat it, maybe you'd find out." He sounded like a parent scolding a child. When she still didn't start eating, he added, "C'mon, you're giving me a complex about my cooking."

"Hey, I helped!" Kennedy reminded him, trying to focus on her meal.

"You're right. You did take the potatoes out of the oven," he said, chuckling.

"I also buttered the corn." Wondering what Braxton had planned for that night, Kennedy delved into her dinner, eating as quickly as she could.

Once they had loaded the dishes into the dishwasher, Kennedy asked, "So what are we going to do?"

"You'll see." He took hold of her hand and led her outside to his truck. Fifteen minutes later they pulled up to a place called The Canyon.

"Where are we?"

"The Canyon."

"So I noticed," Kennedy said dryly. "What kind of place is it?"

Rolling his eyes, Braxton jumped from the truck and came around to open her door. "The place is right there. We will be inside in less than thirty seconds. Surely even you can wait thirty seconds."

"It's not that I can't wait. I'd just like to know what to expect."

"Expect the unexpected."

"I can't believe I'm dating you." Kennedy sulked as Braxton pulled open the door and led her into an indoor rock gym. Glancing around, she beamed. "We're going rock climbing? I've always wanted to do this!"

Braxton smiled at her enthusiasm and congratulated himself for successfully getting Kennedy's mind off Shauna.

✻ ❋ ✻

After Shauna quit, Kennedy's life fell back into a regular pattern. The few hours she was able to spend with Braxton most days seemed to help rejuvenate her spirits. That is, until he dropped her off at the apartment and Kennedy was forced to endure Stacey's uncomfortable silence. Several times, Kennedy attempted to apologize and talk to Stacey, but before she could say more than two words, Stacey always interrupted with, "Don't worry about it," and quickly left the room.

It was after such a discouraging encounter that Kennedy picked up the phone to call her sister Jackie. She needed someone to cheer her up, and Jackie was just the sort of person that could coax a smile from Kennedy.

After five rings, Jackie finally picked up the phone with a hurried, "Hello?"

Kennedy heard what sounded like twenty kids screaming in the background. "Hi, Jack. It's Kennedy." Just picturing Jackie with a house full of kids, made Kennedy laugh.

"This is so not funny," Jackie said.

"What is going on there?"

"I was feeling somewhat energetic this morning and decided to tell my children they could each invite one friend over. Then my neighbor called and asked if she could send over her four children while she ran to the doctor real quick. That was an hour and a half ago. And to make matters worse, it's snowing outside, and we're in the process of repainting our basement, so no children are allowed in the yard or downstairs."

"Sure wish I could be there to help," Kennedy said insincerely.

"I bet you do," Jackie replied, taking a deep breath. "So, what's going on with you?"

"Well, before I called, I thought I was having a bad day. But now that I know yours is much worse, I somehow feel better," Kennedy teased.

Chuckling, Jackie asked, "So what happened with your day?"

"Oh just the usual. Work was boring, and Stacey hates me."

"Wish I could help you out somehow, but I'm afraid there's not much I can do," Jackie replied. "Aren't you going out with Braxton tonight? That ought to cheer you up."

"Oh, he always does, but I'm getting a little worried. The more time I spend with him, the harder I fall."

"And this is a bad thing because . . ."

"Because, what if he's not right for me either? What if I'm setting myself up for heartbreak all over again?"

"What if you're not?"

"Well, that would be great, and I sure wish I could know one way or the other, but Heavenly Father must have a few more important things on His plate right now because I feel like I'm being ignored."

"Yeah, I bet He's forgotten all about you," Jackie joked.

"Funny."

"Tell me, Kennedy. Is there any reason why you think you shouldn't marry Braxton?"

"No."

"I would have to agree. He's pretty amazing. So why don't you just go for it then?"

"Because I did that with Chris, and look where it got me."

"An answer."

"Huh?"

"Frankly, sis, in my opinion the Lord answers prayers in three ways. I've heard it compared to a traffic light. Either it's red for no or green for yes. However, sometimes it can be yellow, as in your situation. And what do you do at a yellow light?"

"Slow down?"

"No, Kenn. What do *you* do at a yellow light?"

"Okay fine, I speed up a little."

"Right, you speed up and go for it. The same thing applies with prayer. You have prayed about this for weeks, hoping for some sort of answer, when what you really need to do is make a decision, go for it, and see what happens. If he's not the right one you'll know—just like you knew with Chris."

"You're probably right," Kennedy conceded. "But that's much easier said than done."

As she hung up the phone with her sister, the apartment door opened and in walked Stacey. She headed for the kitchen, but, when she saw Kennedy, she quickly changed directions and went silently to her bedroom.

Kennedy despised hurting anyone, but, unsure of what else to do, she simply hoped and prayed that one day Stacey would understand and accept her apology.

Thoughts such as these occupied Kennedy's mind that evening as she and Braxton walked hand in hand through Freestone Park. Tightening his grip on her hand, Braxton pulled Kennedy to a stop and turned her to face him. "Hey, what's up?"

"What do you mean?"

"I mean, I've asked you a question three times and gotten no answer, and I'll bet my truck that you can't tell me what that question is."

"Your truck, huh?" Kennedy teased. "That's a pretty risky bet."

"What was the question?"

"I have no idea," she answered honestly, appearing apologetic.

"Good, because I'm rather partial to my truck." Braxton attempted to coax a smile from Kennedy. He was rewarded when a small giggle escaped her mouth.

"What would I do without you?" She smiled as she wrapped her arms around him, hugging him tightly.

"That's what I'd like to get around to talking about someday."

Pulling back slightly, Kennedy's smile was replaced with concern as she said quietly, "I know, but I don't feel like I've received an answer yet. And even if I had, I really don't like the thought of getting engaged and planning a wedding with Stacey hurting so much."

"I know." Braxton sighed as he pulled Kennedy against him. After a few minutes, he released her, and they resumed walking. "So, you still have no idea why Shauna left?"

"No!" exclaimed Kennedy. "And since I can't help being curious, I am completely annoyed."

He chuckled. "I take it you still don't think you can come work for me, huh? I'd like to think that Shauna's resignation releases you from your verbal agreement."

"I made the agreement with the company, not just Shauna. Besides, I really feel like I need to stick around, at least until they hire a replacement for Shauna. For some reason, though, I feel as though I need to be there. Don't ask me why, because it will just lead me back to that lousy curiosity problem. And I'm trying so hard not to wonder."

Laughing, Braxton pulled her into his arms for a quick kiss. "Do you think you can get off a little early on Friday?" he asked.

"I might be able to arrange that," said Kennedy. "Why?"

"I'll remind you that Friday is Valentine's Day, and the rest is a surprise." He released her and reclaimed her hand.

"Great. You realize you've just given me one more thing to be curious about."

✻ ❁ ✻

Waiting for Friday was like waiting for a dial-up Internet connection. When the anticipated day and hour finally arrived, Kennedy couldn't log off her computer fast enough. Her excitement was diminished only slightly when she arrived home to find Stacey watching an old movie on TV. Braxton would be there in less than an hour, and Kennedy dreaded the misery she would undoubtedly see in Stacey's eyes. Mumbling a quick hello, Kennedy fled to her room and hurriedly dressed for the evening. Selecting a soft green V-neck sweater and some black dress pants, she quickly slid on a pair of stylish half boots and studied her reflection in the mirror. Pleased with her ensemble, she carefully reapplied some light makeup and—after only two attempts—managed to clip her hair up in a waterfall of curls down the back of her head. After adding a pair of short, dangly, white gold earrings, Kennedy rubbed some scented lotion on her hands before plopping down on her bed to wait for the doorbell to ring. She had no intention of attempting to make idle conversation with Stacey in the front room.

The doorbell rang at exactly five o'clock. Kennedy grabbed her jacket and headed quickly for the door. To her dismay, Stacey was one step ahead.

"Oh—uh—hi, B. J." Stacey sounded extremely flustered, and Kennedy cringed, staying hidden in her room for a moment.

"Hey, how's it going? I haven't seen you in awhile," Braxton replied easily, letting himself into the apartment and acting as though nothing were wrong.

"I've been a little busy, and you've been preoccupied," Stacey mumbled. "Let me get Kennedy for you."

"So, how's school going?" Braxton asked before she could go anywhere.

"Fine." Stacey stopped and turned around. "If I take a few classes during the summer, I'll be able to apply for nursing school in the fall and hopefully start in January."

"That's great!" Braxton smile warmly. "Any idea about what kind of nurse you'd like to be?"

"Labor and delivery."

"Really?" He sounded surprised.

"Well, the nursery, at any rate. I love babies."

"Well, whatever you decide, you'll be terrific."

"Thanks, B. J." Stacey cocked her head to one side. "So, how's the business?"

"Busy," he replied. "But it's going well. The models we just opened—the ones Kennedy decorated—are selling like hotcakes, and our Albuquerque development is finally starting to pick up a little."

"That's good. Any new land acquisitions?"

"We're looking at a small piece out in east Mesa but haven't purchased it yet."

"Well, I'm sure that when you do, it will also sell like hotcakes."

"That's the hope."

She smiled, almost sadly. "Well, let me get Kennedy for you."

Kennedy started guiltily, knowing she'd been eavesdropping. She was sad and a little jealous to hear how easily B. J. was able to talk to Stacey and wished for the millionth time that someday Stacey would come to forgive her. In addition, Stacey's few remarks to Braxton had made her realize how self-absorbed she'd been the past several weeks. She knew about the development she'd been involved with, for obvious reasons, but she hadn't thought to ask Braxton about any new developments on the horizon or how his New Mexico development was coming along. What a brat she was becoming. Mentally, she kicked herself and resolved to forget about her own troubles and think about someone else for a change. "It's all right, Stacey, I'm here." Kennedy spoke from the far side of the room, slowly making her way toward the door.

Braxton's eyes followed her as she crossed to his side. "We'll see you later, Stace," he said as he opened the door and ushered Kennedy outside, closing it softly behind him.

"You look beautiful." Braxton gazed at her admiringly, taking her in his arms and kissing her briefly.

"Thank you." She smiled up at him as she pulled away and laced her fingers through his. "You look pretty handsome yourself." He was wearing a blue, collared shirt and khaki pants.

They descended the stairs together, and Braxton chuckled. "So, that was a little awkward in there."

Kennedy responded dolefully. "I don't know what else to do. I've given up on trying to talk to her because she avoids me. She completely despises me, and I feel terrible." Shaking her head, Kennedy went on. "There's got to be something I can do to make things right."

"Some things you just can't fix. My feelings for you are unchangeable, so until Stacey learns to accept that and forgive us, nothing is going to change." They had arrived at the truck, and Braxton opened the door for her. Then he jogged around and slid into the driver's seat.

"Stacey did clue me in on one thing tonight, though," Kennedy said regretfully, glancing guiltily at Braxton.

"What's that?" Braxton asked, starting the car.

Kennedy grimaced as she turned to stare out her window. "She reminded me that I've been pathetically self-absorbed these past few weeks." Glancing back in his direction, she reached for his hand. "I'm so sorry, Brax. What can I do to make it up to you?"

Braxton chuckled as he lifted her hand and placed a soft kiss on her knuckles. "I can think of something."

"Oh yeah, what's that?" Kennedy asked.

"I'll give you a hint. It involves a ring and a yes." He winked, making Kennedy laugh. "Hey, it's Valentine's Day. Let's forget all about decisions and Stacey for one night and have some fun—just you and me."

"Sounds like a dream," Kennedy said, eyeing him slyly. "But I'm afraid that in order for me to completely relax and enjoy myself, I'm going to need to know exactly where we are going tonight."

Braxton remained predictably silent, but he did offer her a half smile.

After they had a delicious dinner at The Cheesecake Factory, which was Kennedy's favorite restaurant, Braxton drove them to the Gammage Auditorium on the ASU campus. Casting a curious glance his way as he opened her door, she took his outstretched hand and followed him inside. Her curiosity was finally put to rest when the usher handed them a program for a Jim Brickman concert.

Kennedy looked at him excitedly. "I love Jim Brickman!"

Smiling, Braxton said, "I know. You have every CD he's ever released."

"You are amazing. Do you know that?" Kennedy leaned into him and kissed him lightly.

"I'll take you to all of his concerts if that's the thanks I get."

Laughing, she reached up to kiss him once again, saying, "You don't need to take me to concerts to get that kind of thanks."

Braxton put his hand on the small of her back as he guided her up the rows to find their seats. It was only when Kennedy was seated that she glanced sideways at Braxton and found him still standing, staring at the person sitting on the other side of Kennedy. Raising her eyebrows, Kennedy turned in her seat, only to find an attractive brunette laughing and conversing with her date. Catching people staring out of the corner of her eye, the brunette finally looked over inquisitively at Kennedy and then up at Braxton, where her curiosity turned into shock, followed by a look of complete discomfort. Noting Braxton's grim expression, Kennedy knew something was wrong. An awkward silence filled the air as Braxton stared without speaking, and the brunette looked everywhere but his face. The brunette's date took in the situation and looked to Kennedy for answers. She could only shrug her shoulders and hope that Braxton would come out of his stupor.

Deciding to try to ease the tension, Kennedy placed her hand in Braxton's and gently gave his arm a tug. He resisted at first but finally allowed her to pull him down. His grim expression remained as he sat and stared at the empty stage. Realizing that he wasn't going to say anything to the brunette, Kennedy opted to take matters into her own hands and turned in her seat. "Hi, I'm Kennedy," she said, "a friend of Braxton's. I take it you two know each other?"

Somehow, the brunette looked even more distressed as she fiddled with her program, appearing unsure of what to say. Glancing at her date's raised eyebrows, she finally introduced herself. "I'm Lauren, and this is my husband, Jake." She gestured to the man seated next to her.

"Oh, it's nice to meet you." Kennedy smiled warmly, still curious about Lauren's relationship to Braxton. Was she an old girlfriend? Maybe a friend of Crystal's? Who?

To Kennedy's relief, Jake repeated Kennedy's earlier question, "So how is it you two know each other?"

Glancing back at Braxton, Kennedy noticed he was still looking straight ahead, as if completely oblivious to the conversation going on right next to him. Seeing he was going to be no help, Kennedy's eyes darted back to Lauren, hoping for some sort of explanation.

Finally caving under the pressure of two sets of eyes, Lauren admitted almost grudgingly, "He's my brother."

Kennedy's eyes widened in surprise as Jake appeared stupefied. Thankfully, they were saved from further conversation as the lights dimmed and the announcer came on stage.

Normally, Kennedy would have immersed herself in the concert, but she found herself unable to do that. Instead, she stewed over how to get Braxton to finally talk to his sister. It had been over a decade, and Kennedy considered it providence that Lauren was sitting right next to them. But then Kennedy overheard Jake ask his wife an incredibly disturbing question. "You have a brother?"

Kennedy bit back a heated rebuke to Lauren. It was bad enough she refused to speak to Braxton, but how could she not tell her own husband that she had a brother? Knowing she had a sort of ally in Jake, she decided that as soon as intermission came, she was going to have a word with Braxton's sister.

Unfortunately, the minute the lights turned on, Lauren jumped up, mumbling something about having to use the ladies' restroom. Not willing to let her get away so easily, Kennedy moved to follow, only to be held back by Braxton's sudden death grip on her hand.

"Don't even think about it," he whispered sternly.

"But I need to use the restroom too," Kennedy tried feebly.

"Nice try." Braxton's hold tightened, and she sighed disappointedly.

Seeing Jake out of the corner of her eye, Kennedy decided to have a little chat with him, since she obviously wasn't going after Lauren. He was staring down at his hands, completely preoccupied, so she took a moment to study him. He looked nice enough.

"So how long have you and Lauren been married?"

He glanced at Kennedy and responded, "Four months."

"Oh, wow, that's pretty recent. Congratulations."

"Thanks." He nodded distractedly as his eyes strayed back toward his hands.

"Are you originally from around here?"

"No, actually I'm from a little town outside of Idaho Falls."

"So what brought you here?"

He shrugged. "After I graduated, I landed a job down here. I've lived here for seven years now."

"Do you like it here?"

His forehead crinkled in thought before he responded, "I like it well enough. It has grown on me a lot, but I would still love to move back to Idaho, given the right opportunity. I keep telling Lauren that she'd love it there, but she naturally prefers to stay close to her family."

Kennedy felt Braxton stiffen as Jake realized the bad timing of his comment. Trying to diffuse his comments, he stuttered, "I'm sorry, I didn't mean—"

"Don't worry about it," Braxton said tightly.

Kennedy looked from Braxton to Jake, rolling her eyes at Braxton's behavior. The way he felt about his sister was understandable, but the way he was treating Jake was not. After all, Jake had no idea Lauren even had a brother. He was an innocent bystander in this whole family drama, and he shouldn't be treated rudely. Relinquishing her hold on Braxton's hand, Kennedy turned fully toward Jake, engaging him once again in conversation.

"So, what degree did you study in college?"

"Business Management. I'm actually taking some night classes, and I'll have my master's degree in another year."

"Hey, that's great." Kennedy smiled kindly. "Good luck with that."

"Thanks. It seems like it's taken forever, but the end is finally in sight, and I'm grateful for that."

"I'll bet. So, where did you graduate from?"

Looking a little uncomfortable with the question, he responded hesitantly. "I went to a private institution in Utah. It's called Brigham Young University."

Kennedy was unable to mask her surprise. "You went to BYU?" Even Braxton seemed to perk up and look interested.

"You're familiar with the school?"

"Just a little. That's where I graduated from."

Before Jake could respond, Braxton interrupted. "You mean you're LDS?"

Jake looked slightly sheepish as he replied, "Yeah. I know how your family feels about the Mormons, but Lauren and I fell head over heels. It caused some major concerns for your family, but they've accepted me, and we just have a mutual agreement not to talk about religion."

Kennedy could tell that Braxton was fighting for control of his emotions as Jake's words sunk in. Seeing the muscles work in his jaw, she gently reached over and grabbed his hand.

"Listen," Jake said. "Until tonight, I honestly had no idea Lauren even had a brother. I have no idea why she's never told me and why we've never met, but I intend to get to the bottom of things as soon as we get home."

"Yeah, and while you're at it," Braxton said bitterly, "you can go ahead and ask them exactly why they accepted you and disowned me and my father." With that, Braxton stood and grabbed Kennedy's hand, obviously intent on leaving the concert. Throwing an apologetic glance over her shoulder toward Jake, she followed Braxton out of the auditorium.

As soon as they were seated in the truck, Kennedy reached over and stayed Braxton's hand from starting the ignition. "Brax, I'm so sorry." Scooting over, Kennedy wrapped her arm around Braxton's and laid her head on his broad shoulder, offering him what comfort she could.

Letting the quiet permeate the air around them, Braxton struggled to get his emotions under control. He was so sick of being angry with his family. Just when things were starting to go right in his life, he had to bump into his sister. Would he ever be able to leave it all behind? Having Kennedy by his side helped a great deal. If only she would stay there forever. What if she decided that he wasn't right for her either? He'd never voiced his concerns aloud, not wanting to stress Kennedy, but in the dark recesses of his mind he did have anxiety. Lots of anxiety. Quite frankly, he was petrified. He wasn't sure he could handle losing Kennedy. She was like an anesthetic, erasing so much pain in his life. But he also knew that any day, any moment, she might come to the conclusion that he wasn't what the Lord wanted for her either, and the thought made him want to vomit. Noticing the excess moisture in his eyes, Braxton turned his head away from Kennedy and stared out the window, blinking rapidly. Some Valentine's Day.

Lifting her head from his shoulder, Kennedy reached for his chin with her free hand. Slowly, she guided his head around to face her. Mistaking the reason for his tears, Kennedy cut through the silence and reasoned quietly, "Has it occurred to you that they accepted Jake into their family because they realized the huge mistake they made with you and your father? Don't you think that now may be a good time to finally make amends and move on?"

Braxton sighed in frustration. "Kennedy, I—"

"After all, I want our children to have two families, not just mine."

Ignoring the first two questions, Braxton focused on her last remark. "Our children?" A single fleck of hope sparked in his eyes, causing his heart to stop. He stared at her intently, willing her to say the words he most wanted to hear.

Realizing her Freudian slip, Kennedy guiltily tried to find an excuse for her comment. Before she could speak, however, a sudden warm, peaceful feeling engulfed her body, warming her from head to toe. Tears of gratitude sprang to her eyes as she smiled at Braxton in wonder. *Thank you, Father. Thank you.* "I think I just got my answer. Actually, I know I just got my answer." Squealing like a little girl, Kennedy removed her hand from his and threw both of her arms around his neck. "I get to marry you!" she whispered in his ear.

Shifting her over to sit sideways on his lap, Braxton's hold on her tightened, as if he were afraid it was all a dream, and she would disappear if he let go. The self-pity he had been experiencing only minutes before swiftly fled. "Are you sure?" He was almost afraid to ask the question.

"I've never been more sure of anything." She smiled, placing her hands on either side of his face. "I love you and definitely want to marry you."

"I love you too." He brought his lips to hers in a tender kiss. His mouth moved across hers slowly, wanting to savor the taste of her.

Gradually, his kiss traveled down her throat and to her neck. His hands removed the clip from her hair as his fingers ran through her soft, silky curls. Kennedy's hands also found their way to the back of his neck and up into his hair. She reveled in the sensation of being thoroughly kissed. His lips found their way back to hers, and the kiss deepened for a moment before he broke away, kissing her lightly on the forehead and hugging her tightly.

"Wow." Kennedy smiled almost shyly. "If you promise to kiss me like that at least once a day, I promise to be the best wife you could ever have."

Braxton pulled her close again. "It's a deal."

Chapter 15

Kennedy! What are you doing home so soon? It's not even eleven!" Mia exclaimed as Kennedy walked through the door into their apartment. Ever since Mia had quit her job to go to school, Kennedy saw a lot more of her sweet roommate.

Kennedy laughed at Mia's obvious distress. "Let's just say we had an interesting night."

"You didn't break up, did you?" asked Mia, her voice filled with concern.

Glancing quickly at Stacey, Kennedy answered, "Uh, no, we didn't. We just ran into one of Braxton's sisters."

Miraculously, Stacey perked up and actually spoke. "Which one?"

Masking her surprise, Kennedy plopped down on the love seat, taking full advantage of the opportunity to actually talk to Stacey again. "Lauren."

"What happened?" Stacey was probably the only one who could understand the drama of Braxton running into his sister. Coupling this awareness with her natural interest, Stacey had finally let her guard down, at least for the moment.

"She happened to be sitting right next to me at the concert we went to tonight."

"You're kidding. How awkward was that?"

"Very awkward, especially since all Braxton could do was glare at her."

"I can only imagine. So, what did you do?"

"Well, I couldn't just sit there, wondering all night, so I finally turned to her and asked what her name was and how she and Braxton knew each other."

"You didn't."

"Well, I had no idea she was his sister."

Mia finally entered the conversation, obviously confused. "You've never met his family?"

Thankfully, Stacey answered quickly before Kennedy could think of how to explain. "No, Mia. B. J.'s family basically disowned him and his father years ago."

"Why?"

"Because they joined the Mormon Church."

"Oh," was all Mia said before both she and Stacey stared back at Kennedy, silently urging her to continue.

"She finally introduced herself—as well as her husband."

"Lauren's married?" Stacey practically squealed.

Kennedy nodded. "As of four months ago."

"That's crazy!" exclaimed Stacey. "And Braxton had no idea?"

"None," replied Kennedy. "And to add insult to injury, her husband, Jake, not only didn't know Lauren had a brother, but it just so happens that he is a member of our church."

Stacey's eyes practically popped out of her head. "Jake's a Mormon? Lauren told you that?"

"No way. Jake did after Lauren tactfully excused herself during the intermission," Kennedy answered wryly. "So, as I'm sure you can imagine, once Braxton learned that news, we didn't stick around for the remainder of the concert. He didn't even bother to explain anything to Jake—we just up and left."

"Well, you can't blame him for that, can you?"

"Of course not," Kennedy said, sighing. "But I'm just crazy enough to think that since they've accepted Jake, maybe Braxton and his family can finally let bygones be bygones."

Stacey chuckled mirthlessly. "You actually think B. J. will try to talk to them again? I'm afraid that he has way too much pride for that—as does his family, obviously, or they would have invited him to the wedding, or at the very least told Jake about B. J."

"I know," Kennedy agreed. "So what can I do?"

"Are you joking?" Stacey asked, astounded. "If you tried to interfere, B. J. would kill you!"

"Oh I know he wouldn't be happy about my interference, but I can't just stand around and pretend that he doesn't have a family."

"Why should you care?" Stacey asked sharply.

"Listen, Stace," Kennedy replied sorrowfully. "I know you must hate me and think I'm the biggest hypocrite alive—which is understandable, because I feel like one. Honestly, though, even though I was starting to care about him, I would have never done anything about it. In fact, I had no idea he harbored any feelings for me until Christmas. I feel miserable for what we've put you through, and I will understand if you can never forgive me. I also need to tell you . . ." Kennedy hesitated as her eyes worriedly probed Stacey's. "We've decided to get married."

"You're getting married?" Mia squealed with delight and rushed to give Kennedy a hug. "I can't believe it! This is so exciting!"

"Thanks, Mia," Kennedy said slowly, wishing Mia would curb her enthusiasm a bit. Glancing Stacey's way, Kennedy willed her to say something—anything.

When Stacey finally looked up, Kennedy could see tears running down her cheeks. Not knowing what else to say, Kennedy went to Stacey, tentatively placing her hand on Stacey's arm. "I'm so sorry, Stace. I never set out to steal Braxton from you, I promise. Please don't hate me."

Stacey shook her head, blinking rapidly. "It's okay. I won't say that I'm not hurting badly, but I'll get over it someday. Deep down, I've always known that he only cared for me as a sister, and it was wrong to blame you for my broken heart. I'm just so tired of being angry and sad all the time. I decided a while ago that I needed to grow up, I just didn't know what to say or do. From now on, I will try really hard to be happy for you and B. J."

Kennedy smiled and hugged her roommate. "Thank you, Stacey. That means so much to me."

Nodding slowly, Stacey replied shakily. "Just don't expect me to help with any wedding stuff."

Kennedy and Mia both laughed before Mia exclaimed, "Oh, I forgot! Kenn, someone called for you while you were gone."

"Who?" She couldn't imagine anyone calling for her on Valentine's night.

"I forget his name, but he did say that he's flying out here."

"What?"

"I wrote his name on the pad by the phone."

Kennedy rose quickly as her brain worked to come up with some sort of explanation. The name she saw written caused her heart to stop.

"Chris is coming here?" she murmured to herself.

"Yeah, it was a really strange call," Mia explained. "He asked if you were here, and I told him you were out with your boyfriend for Valentine's Day. He mumbled something about catching the earliest flight out here before hanging up."

"He what?" Kennedy screeched.

"Sorry," Mia said, looking concerned. "That's all he told me."

Stacey finally chimed in. "So, are you going to tell us who Chris is?"

Realizing she had never told her roommates anything about Chris, Kennedy was forced to explain. "He's a guy I was engaged to last year."

"You were engaged?" Mia and Stacey practically shouted in unison.

"It's a long story."

"Well," Stacey stated matter-of-factly, tapping the cushion next to her on the sofa. "You did get home early."

Kennedy sat down gingerly and told them the entire Chris saga. When she was finished with her narrative, Stacey was staring at her wide-eyed. "Wow, that's some story, especially now that he's on his way to come see you." Stacey surprised Kennedy by giggling. "Boy, is Becca going to be mad she missed all this."

Kennedy smiled wryly, glad to see Stacey smile, even if it was at her expense. "Well, I guess there's nothing I can do but wait and see what happens." She started to get up from the couch and head to her room to change when Stacey halted her with one final question.

"Hey, Kenn, do you still have feelings for Chris?"

Kennedy thought about the question for a moment before answering. "I'm not sure. He was the first guy I fell in love with and, to be honest, until the last few months I always wished he would somehow come back into my life and things would work out between us. I honestly have no idea how I'll feel when and if I actually see him face to face. I know that a part of me will always care about him because he's such a wonderful person. But I also know that I didn't meet Braxton by chance. Somehow, I'm more in love with him than I ever was with Chris, and I also know that marrying him is the right thing for me to do."

"How do you know?" Mia asked with open curiosity.

Shaking her head slowly, Kennedy replied thoughtfully, "It's just this amazing feeling I got when Braxton and I talked about getting married. It's hard to explain, but I know it was the Spirit testifying to me that we were making the right choice. I have never felt so good or happy or peaceful, and I never want to forget that feeling."

Stacey eyed her skeptically while Mia appeared more in awe. But neither spoke, so Kennedy quickly said good night and headed for her room.

✲ ✲ ✲

The following day, Kennedy pushed Chris to the back of her mind while Braxton took her shopping for an engagement ring. They were gone most of the day and visited what felt like every store in the Phoenix area before they finally came to a small store called Treasures. It was there that Kennedy found the perfect ring. It was a simple, white gold band with a beautiful round diamond centered in a beveled setting. Kennedy loved it immediately, and since it fit her finger perfectly they were able to take it with them as they left the store.

Braxton grinned as he buckled himself into the truck. "Now I just need to think of a way to formally propose."

"But you already did—during Christmas break, remember?" Kennedy answered back.

"Yeah, but that didn't count. I was just putting out feelers, to see how you'd react when I did get around to actually proposing. Besides, I haven't even asked for your father's permission."

"It does too count, and believe me, you have my dad's permission. Did you not see the approval in his eyes Christmas morning when he caught you kissing me under the mistletoe? He will be so happy not to have to buy me any more power tools," Kennedy reminded him, holding out her hand. "Now, please, if you will, hand over my ring."

Braxton laughed, shaking his head at Kennedy. "All right, you win. But we will call your parents together, so I can clear it with them both. Deal?"

"Deal." She smiled happily as he opened the box and placed the ring on her finger, following it up with a lingering kiss.

✻❉✻

Later that same evening, Braxton and Kennedy walked into her apartment, laughing together about their day, when Kennedy stopped suddenly, causing Braxton to career into her.

"Kennedy, what in the . . . ?" The words died in Braxton's mouth when he saw some guy staring at Kennedy apprehensively.

"Chris," she said, almost reverently. "You're here."

"I'm here."

Kennedy stood rooted to the spot. "Uh, I'm not sure what to say."

"There's a first," Braxton mumbled from behind her, attempting to dispel some of the tension.

Chris's piercing gaze considered Braxton carefully. "Do you mind if I talk to you alone for a minute?" he asked Kennedy.

Kennedy followed his gaze and turned her head, catching Braxton's eyes. With a pleading look, she placed her hand softly on his forearm. "Hey, do you mind if Chris and I go for a walk?"

He shook his head solemnly, stepping aside and clearing the way to the front door.

She gave a small smile of thanks. Chris led the way out the front door, and Kennedy turned around and blew a kiss Braxton's way before closing the door behind her.

Coming to his senses, Braxton saw Mia, Stacey, and Becca gawking at him, obviously waiting for him to speak. Not wanting to disappoint them, he tried to sound calm. "Anyone up for a game of spades?"

The three girls burst into giggles and agreed. Mia jumped up to make some hot chocolate, and Stacey grabbed some cards from the top of the coat closet. Trying to keep his worries at bay, Braxton partnered up with Stacey and focused on the game.

✳ ❀ ✳

"It's been awhile," Kennedy said lamely as they started on their walk.

"Too long," he stated pointedly. Chris was rarely serious, and Kennedy had no idea what to say to him.

After a few minutes of extremely uncomfortable silence, she asked the question that had been on her mind since she heard he was coming: "Why did you come?"

Taking a deep breath, he turned his sullen eyes on her before explaining. "I haven't been able to get you off my mind. I've spent the last eight months hoping that the timing was just off. In November, I finally started to ask my company about opportunities to relocate."

"Are you unhappy with your job?"

"They recently opened an office in Phoenix."

"Oh."

"Finally, last week, they told me there was an opening and asked if I was interested. I flew down here for a day to interview and was offered the job a couple days later. That's when I called you."

"Have you given them an answer yet?"

"Nope," he said, breathing heavily. "I sort of wanted to talk to you first."

"Wow," Kennedy replied. "I'm not sure what to say."

"I'm not sure anything you have to say is what I'll want to hear, so it's probably for the best."

This brought a small smile from Kennedy, but it soon faded. "I'm afraid some things have changed," she said carefully.

"I noticed." He glanced meaningfully at her left ring finger.

"I'm engaged."

"Got that." He nodded numbly. "Does it feel right this time?"

"Yes."

"Okay then. I guess that's what I needed to know."

"I'm so sorry, Chris." Kennedy felt horrible. Was she ever going to stop hurting people? Relationships weren't supposed to be so complicated. You fall in love with someone, and he falls in love with you.

You get married. Done. Why couldn't her life be so simple? She had hurt Chris, then Stacey, and now Chris again. She felt like a complete jerk. "What are you going to do about the job?"

He laughed mirthlessly. "I'm not sure. The funny thing is that I applied for it because of you, but after the interview I realized that I might actually like the change. It would be a lot more challenging and rewarding. "

"Sounds like a good opportunity."

"Yeah, but to be honest, I'm not sure I can live here in Phoenix knowing that you're out of my reach."

Kennedy nodded her understanding. "Have you prayed about it?"

"Yeah, and I was feeling pretty good about it, which is why I got to hoping that you and I would . . ." he hesitated, "well, you know."

"Yeah, I know." Kennedy had to chuckle sardonically at the irony of life. "I used to wish for the same thing."

"But not anymore," Chris said as he looked off into the distance.

"There's someone better for you out there, Chris—I know it. You just need to find her. And in the meantime, just factor me out of your decision and decide where you need to be."

"I wish I had your faith, Kennedy." His tone was somber. "I've always loved that about you. Even though it took you away from me."

She had to blink to keep the tears from her eyes. "You are an amazing person, and I will always care about you, but I do love Braxton. He's right for me, and he's a good guy."

"He'd better be," Chris muttered. The wonderfully familiar teasing lilt returned to his voice as he grabbed her arm and turned them both back toward her apartment. "We'd better get back before your fiancé gets too jealous."

"Braxton isn't the jealous type."

"Believe me, when it comes to a fiancée out on a walk with her former fiancé, every guy is the jealous type."

"Well, when you put it that way . . ." Kennedy laughed. "You know, if you think about it, this situation is really quite ridiculous." She briefly explained about Stacey.

Chris laughed. "Well, I'm glad I'm not the only one with a broken heart."

"Oh, I'm sorry. Forgive me for making light of our situation."

"No, please don't be sorry. I'd much rather laugh about my misfortunes than cry about them."

Spontaneously, she reached up and gave him a brotherly hug. "That's one thing I've always admired about you." Kennedy smiled up at him. "You're the one hurting, and yet *you* are trying to make *me* feel better."

"I know. What's wrong with me?"

Kennedy laughed out loud. "I think I need to introduce you to Stacey. Maybe you could make her feel better too."

"Why not?" he joked. "At least we have something in common. We could start our own support group or something."

Kennedy was laughing heartily as they arrived back at her apartment and let themselves back in. They found the others ensconced around the coffee table, playing cards and sipping hot chocolate. Leading Chris into the room, Kennedy officially introduced him to Braxton and asked everyone to make room for two more.

By the end of the night, it seemed as though everyone was in harmony with each other. Kennedy was amazed with how easy it was to relegate Chris into the friend category. She had genuine affection for him, but nothing like she felt for Braxton, and she hoped that one day he'd feel the same way. She was so grateful for Chris's attitude and for Braxton's ability to treat him as a friend. Even Stacey seemed genuinely happy for the first time in months.

Later that evening, the four roommates stayed up late talking lightheartedly about their fun night. After the conversation had died down, Stacey spoke up, almost shyly, referring her question to Kennedy. "So, now that you've seen him, do you still have any feelings for Chris?"

Kennedy considered Stacey's question before answering. "I will always care about him. I mean, now that you guys have met him, how could you not like him, right? But now that I know Braxton, I realize that he's a much better fit for me than Chris ever was. It just goes to show you that the Lord really knows what He's doing."

For the first time, when religion was mentioned, Stacey appeared thoughtful rather than cynical as she nodded her understanding. After a minute or two, though, she timidly asked, "So, do you think Chris will end up taking the job and moving here?"

"I think he might. He told me he felt pretty good about the offer and was excited about the prospect of this job. I just hope I don't keep him from accepting it if this is what he really wants," Kennedy answered honestly. "Why do you ask?"

Stacey didn't have to answer. The blush on her cheeks gave her away.

Becca pounced immediately. "You like him!" she accused, causing Kennedy and Mia to burst into laughter.

"I do not!" Stacey shouted unconvincingly, pushing her face into the throw pillow on her lap to hide her embarrassment.

"Well, why wouldn't you?" asked Mia. "He is really cute."

"And a good kisser," Kennedy added with a giggle, loving how happy Stacey appeared.

"Kennedy!" All three roommates exclaimed in unison, shocked by her pronouncement yet laughing hysterically.

❁ Chapter 16 ❁

KENNEDY RANG THE doorbell quickly, before she lost her nerve. Her stomach was in knots, and she was beginning to feel nauseated, but she wasn't about to back down now.

"May I help you?" A woman in her late fifties answered the door. She was a petite woman with dark hair and light eyes. Kennedy was surprised by the resemblance.

Trying to remember the speech she had rehearsed earlier, Kennedy attempted to clear her head as the woman watched her curiously.

"Hi. You don't know me, but my name is Kennedy Jackson." She extended her hand in salutation. "You must be Mrs. Taylor."

The woman's eyes narrowed as she looked Kennedy up and down. Her hands remained at her side. "On the contrary, young lady. I do know you. And for the record, I haven't gone by Mrs. Taylor for many years. My name is Adelle Hamilton."

Nonplussed, Kennedy racked her brain for a polite answer. "I take it Lauren has told you about me."

"She has," Adelle said matter-of-factly. "What I can't understand, though, is why you are here."

Kennedy looked sadly down at her hands. She wasn't sure what she had hoped for, but it certainly wasn't the cold reception she was getting. Perhaps Braxton was right. Maybe his mother and sisters would never be able to reconcile their differences. How could any mother be so callous toward her only son? Kennedy wasn't sure she would ever understand, and a certain amount of anger surged through her as she squared her shoulders and looked Adelle straight in the eye. "I just thought you might want to know that your only son is getting married—to me." She stopped to let the words sink in, before continuing somewhat curtly, "And in answer to your question, I have to admit that I wanted to meet my future mother-in-law for myself."

The woman appeared bewildered by Kennedy's candor. Not wanting to completely offend her, Kennedy took a deep breath and continued more calmly, "Listen, I know you have given up on Braxton because he's a Mormon, and I'm sure you have your reasons. What I would like to understand is how you can welcome a son-in-law who's also LDS into your home, but not your own son. Braxton has done so much good with his life, despite the hardships he's gone through, and he's an amazing person—someone you should be desperately proud of. How can you not want to know him? He loves you and your daughters, and he's too proud to admit it, but he needs you. He's already lost his father, so please don't be lost to him too."

Seeing a small pool of tears form in Adelle's eyes gave Kennedy a reason to hope. When Adelle stepped aside and opened the door wider, nodding for Kennedy to come in, Kennedy couldn't help but tear up as well. "Thank you for not throwing me out." Her future mother-in-law chuckled.

The two women chatted the entire afternoon and early into the evening before Kennedy glanced at her watch with a gasp. "Oh, dear. Brax was supposed to pick me up an hour ago at my apartment. He's going to be worried sick." Kennedy rushed to pick up her purse from the floor. "And it's not as though I'm going to tell him where I've been."

Adelle smiled warmly. "Thank you for stopping by. I know it wasn't easy for you, but I am so glad you did."

"Thanks for your advice." Kennedy grinned. "I just need to work up my courage a bit and figure out how to get him over here tonight without his hating me in the process."

"Oh, I think you are far more courageous than you give yourself credit for. And if you can find a way to get my son to forgive his stupid mother, I will be forever grateful."

❋ ✿ ❋

Kennedy rushed up her apartment steps and flung open the door, only to find Stacey and Becca seated at the kitchen table, enjoying spaghetti for dinner. "Where's Braxton?" Kennedy blurted.

"Oh, he called over an hour ago to let you know he got stuck at the office," Becca replied flippantly. "He said he'd try you on your cell."

"I forgot to bring it with me. It's still in my room."

"Ah!" Stacey exclaimed, as if she'd had an epiphany. "*That* is the noise we've been hearing." She smiled. "You are one popular girl this evening."

As if on cue, a faint sound of "Santa Claus is Coming to Town" came from the other room, and Kennedy rushed to retrieve her phone. She snatched it up and tried to calm her rapid breathing. "Hello?"

"Kennedy, are you okay? Where have you been?" Braxton asked worriedly.

"I'm so sorry," Kennedy responded. "I had some things to do that took me longer than I thought, and I forgot to bring my phone with me."

"For crying out loud, please try and remember your phone from now on. You scared me."

Kennedy smiled at Braxton's reprimand, before responding, "Yes, Daddy."

"Ha, ha," Braxton said sheepishly. "So, what are you doing right now?"

"Talking to my handsome and charming fiancé."

"And don't you forget it," he quipped. "Hey, do you mind coming over to my office to pick me up? I should be finished by the time you get here."

"Sure." Kennedy smiled. He'd never asked her to pick him up before. Grabbing her purse and shoving her cell phone inside, she headed back to the door.

"Where are you headed?" Becca asked.

"Braxton's running late, so I'm going to pick him up."

"Okay, see you." They both waved good-bye.

Fifteen minutes later, Kennedy poked her head into Braxton's office, smiling at him bent over his desk studying some papers. "Hey, good-lookin'."

Braxton's head popped up, a grin spreading across his face. "Aren't you a sight for sore eyes? That was quick," he commented.

"Believe it or not, I hit every green light, and there was no traffic on the freeway."

"You must be living right."

"But of course."

He smiled before asking, "I wonder if you would mind helping me with a few things before we get some dinner?"

Glancing at her watch and biting her lip, Kennedy wondered how she would manage to pull him away from work and get him to his mother's home.

Noticing her gesture, Braxton asked, "Or do you need to be somewhere?"

Wondering how to answer the question, Kennedy decided to be somewhat honest with him. "Actually we need to be somewhere. And don't ask where—it's a surprise."

"I don't like surprises."

"You'll like this one," Kennedy lied uneasily. She only hoped Braxton would still want to marry her after the night was over.

"How can you be sure?" he teased.

"Why can't you just trust me?" Kennedy arched her eyebrows.

"You've never given me reason to," he stated matter-of-factly, and then belied his statement with a grin. "Okay, fine," he said with resignation. "How much time do we have before we need to leave?"

"Half an hour, tops."

"Okay then, here's the plan. You give me twenty minutes of your undivided attention—"

"You always have my undivided attention," Kennedy interrupted.

"—and then we'll grab a sandwich, and you can take me wherever the heck you want."

"Agreed."

"Good." Braxton thrust the papers he had been studying in her direction. "I just received the newest floor plans for some homes we will be starting in the next six months. I'm not crazy about the layout, but we have to keep the square-footage and footprint basically the same. Any ideas?"

Kennedy's eyes lit up at the challenge, and she excitedly spent the next twenty minutes calling out suggestions. They were able to change one floor plan to Braxton's satisfaction before they had to leave. Kennedy made sure to grab the remaining pages and promised to look them over during the weekend.

As promised, Braxton bought them both sandwiches, and then Kennedy insisted on being the one to drive as they walked out of the fast-food place.

"Can't you just tell me which streets to turn on? I promise to follow your directions." Braxton pleaded.

"Do you not trust my driving skills, Brax?" teased Kennedy.

"Only about as much as I trust you."

"You just earned yourself the back seat, mister."

Braxton chuckled as he opened the driver's door for Kennedy and then jumped in the passenger door with a smile. "I promise to behave, if you'll just let me sit next to you." He grabbed her hand and held it tightly.

"All right then, but only if you promise to close your eyes until we get there."

"Not on your life."

"I figured that was a long shot."

Braxton chuckled as he held Kennedy's hand, determined to figure out where they were going before they got there.

As Kennedy drove along, her hand began to tremble in nervousness as they neared the street where Braxton's mother now lived. Thankfully, Adelle had moved five years earlier, so Braxton had no idea where they were going. Or so Kennedy thought. The minute they turned down Adelle's particular street, though, she felt Braxton stiffen as he pulled his hand away from hers.

"Kennedy, will you please tell me where we're going?" His voice was strained, and she could tell he was upset.

Pulling up in front of Adelle's house, Kennedy turned off the ignition and turned to Braxton. "How did you know she lived here?"

Braxton's jaw was working overtime, trying to fight the anger surging through him. "Please take me home," he said, ignoring her question.

"Not until you talk to her."

He looked at her incredulously, feeling completely betrayed. "Kennedy, how could you?" Braxton voice was like steel. "You know the way I feel and the way my family feels. How can you expect me to just walk in and feed myself to the wolves?"

"She's not a wolf, Brax," Kennedy said quietly as she quickly blinked the tears from her eyes. "She's an incredibly sweet woman who feels terrible about the way she's treated you over the years, and she just wants your forgiveness."

"You don't know her," he replied bitterly.

"I met her this afternoon," she revealed quietly.

"You what?" he practically shouted, shaking his head in anger. "How dare you get involved in something that is none of your business? You can't fix this, Kennedy!"

"None of my business?" Kennedy's tone escalated to match his. "How can you say this is none of my business? You're going to be my husband, for crying out loud. And the wonderful lady inside that home—your mother—is going to be our children's grandmother."

Braxton took a deep breath, trying to calm himself down. "Maybe we got engaged prematurely." His anger made him want to hurt her like she'd hurt him.

She could only stare at him in amazement before whispering, "Please don't say that."

Suddenly their argument was interrupted with a quiet knock on the window. They both turned to find Adelle standing outside Braxton's window, looking extremely nervous. Braxton slowly opened his door and got out, glaring at Kennedy before practically slamming the door behind him. Feeling tears burning in her eyes, Kennedy immediately turned on the ignition and sped away. She drove straight back to her apartment and found Stacey alone on the couch studying.

"Stacey, do you mind helping me with something for a minute?" Kennedy asked, trying to keep her voice from shaking.

Stacey noticed Kennedy's red eyes and tear-stained cheeks. "Kennedy, what's the matter?"

Trying hard to fight another onslaught of tears, Kennedy eventually gave up and sank down into the love seat. "I've gone and screwed things up royally."

"What are you talking about?"

"I went to see Braxton's mom without him knowing and then arranged to bring him by tonight to see her as well."

"You did what?"

"You sound like Braxton," sniffed Kennedy, looking at Stacey sadly. "He basically told me that we got engaged too quickly, and I think he wants to call it all off."

"Where is he now?"

"I left him at Adelle's house."

"You mean to tell me he's with his mom right now?"

"I'm afraid he didn't have much choice," admitted Kennedy. "She knocked on the car window when we were arguing, and of course he had to get out and confront her. Initially, I was planning on sticking around with them—Adelle wanted me there as a middleman, so to speak. But I was a complete wreck by that point, so I just drove off."

"You did what?" Stacey repeated incredulously.

"You already said that."

"Kennedy, are you crazy?"

Closing her eyes, Kennedy responded resolutely, "I think there is a distinct possibility that I am, Stace."

Out of nowhere, Stacey burst into laughter. Kennedy stared at her in wonder, thinking that Stacey had gone completely mad as well. "What is so funny?"

"I'm sorry. It's just that I was trying to picture Braxton, standing there with his estranged mother while you drove off and left him stranded. It's so outrageous that it's actually funny," Stacey explained.

"Well, I'm glad that you're getting a kick out of Braxton breaking up with me, because I am certainly not."

"For pete's sake, Kennedy," Stacey said, sounding like a mother talking to her overly dramatic daughter. "He's not going to break up with you. That boy is head over heels for you. With any luck, he'll finally sort things out with his mom and come back to you, begging for forgiveness."

"I think I should have waited until we were married before I tried something like this. That way, he'd be stuck with me forever whether he liked it or not," Kennedy said with a small smile. Unfortunately, the smile faded quickly and she glanced at Stacey sadly. "Now, if you wouldn't mind following me back to Adelle's house, I'd be grateful. I need to leave Braxton's truck out front and then go pick my car up from his office."

✳ ❀ ✳

Braxton couldn't believe it when he saw Kennedy drive away. Now how was he supposed to get out of here? It angered him beyond belief that Kennedy would do something like this.

Closing his eyes, he took a deep breath and turned an angry look on his mother, waiting for her to say something.

Adelle only shrugged and said, "Well, if it's any consolation, your fiancée tricked us both." She watched the truck round the corner at the far end of the street. Glancing back at her son, she explained, "She was supposed to stay and give me moral support."

"Some fiancée she turned out to be," Braxton muttered under his breath. At that moment, he wasn't sure he would ever be able to forgive Kennedy.

"Oh, come now," Adelle said abruptly. "She actually did us both a favor. We've been needing to talk for some time now." Glancing warily at Braxton, she added, "Will you please come inside, if for no other reason than to call for a ride?"

Seeing no way out, Braxton silently led the way to the house. Upon reaching the front door, he stopped and allowed Adelle to precede him inside.

"May I please use your phone?" Braxton stood stiffly in the foyer, his hands shoved in his pockets.

"You may," Adelle said calmly. "But not until you hear me out." She gestured for Braxton to take a seat in the front room.

"It's no wonder you and Kennedy got along so well," he drawled, obeying her silent command by parking himself in the nearest armchair.

"She is a dear, isn't she?" Adelle laughed, sitting opposite him on a sofa. "How did she say it? Something about how you're someone

I should be desperately proud of and how can I not want to know you?" Braxton remained silent, so Adelle continued. "The truth of the matter is that she is right. I do want to know you, Braxton."

Sighing, she sank back against the couch cushions and looked toward the ceiling before she began her story. "I was so angry with your father back then. We had something special between us, and he went and changed it all. We were both at home that day those elders of your church dropped by. Your father invited them in, and we both listened. After that, Jade kept inviting them back, saying he wanted to learn more. I thought what they were saying was crazy and told Jade I didn't want them back in our home.

"Did he listen to me? No. Of course, I didn't know it at the time, because he scheduled the meetings during my weekly aerobics class. Did he even explain to me why he wanted to listen? No. He went on meeting them behind my back, even drawing you into them as well. And one day, out of the blue, he announced that you both were getting baptized.

"I had no idea what he was talking about. It had been about two months since the missionaries first came to our house, and I had put it out of my mind. When he explained that you were both joining the Church, I was livid. How could he go behind my back, brainwash my son, and join a church I despised? To me, it was a horrible, unforgivable betrayal. He might as well have said, 'I don't love you anymore.' I was deeply wounded, and I retaliated with anger. It was much easier to be angry than to deal with the pain.

"Braxton, I had a lot of pride—still do, in fact. I told him that if he went through with the baptism, our marriage was over. And that if you followed in his footsteps, you may as well join him. But you already know that part. He tried to convince me that he still loved me and that we could still have a wonderful and happy marriage—that he wasn't asking me to join the Church, but I wouldn't listen. I gave him the ultimatum, wanting him to prove he loved me." Adelle's eyes were moist with unshed tears. "He didn't, though, as you remember. You both just went right ahead and got baptized without hesitation. I was so hurt and angry that I filed divorce papers immediately.

"My pride, Braxton, was unstoppable. It stopped me from forgiving him—from forgiving you. Whenever I heard either of your voices over the phone, all those lousy feelings of betrayal surfaced with a vengeance. I couldn't deal with it, so I refused to speak to either of you. Lauren and Stefani only heard my warped side of the story, so, in a way, I'm at fault for them cutting you off as well. I couldn't take the chance of losing them too, should they take your side."

The tears began to fall in full force as she recalled in barely a whisper, "I didn't know, Braxton." Her voice gained strength as she went on. "I didn't know about Jade that last time you called. I heard about it several days later from a friend. I even missed the funeral. His death nearly killed me. I always held a hope in my heart that he still loved me enough to give up this new religion of his and return to me, bringing you back as well. But then I discovered he was gone—forever. I fell into a depression. Lauren and Stefani made me see a psychiatrist, and it took me over two years to start to recover. But at that point I couldn't just call you up. Not after the way I treated you. I convinced myself you were better off without me in your life—that I was a poor excuse for a mother, and you deserved so much more.

"And then Lauren met Jake, and oh, what a déjà vu nightmare that was. Lauren couldn't keep herself from falling in love with him. When she found out he was a Mormon, she tried to call it quits, but he wasn't about to let that happen, and within two short months they were engaged. I'll never forget the day I met him. Lauren had warned him not to talk about his religion to me, but did he listen?" Adelle smiled through her tears, recalling the memory. "He walked right up to me with that charming smile of his, held out his hand, and announced, 'Hi, I'm Jake Barister, and I'm a Mormon.'

"Kennedy reminded me so much of that experience today when she showed up on my doorstep." Adelle smiled. "After the initial shock of it all, I refused to make the same mistake I made with you and your father. I welcomed Jake into what was left of our family with open arms. I only made him promise to not talk to me about his religion. In a way, I needed Jake. He inadvertently helped me to finally forgive and let go of my anger."

Braxton finally decided to speak. "Why didn't you ever tell Jake about me?" He leaned forward in his chair, holding his head with his hands as he stared down at the carpet.

Adelle's eyes clouded over. "That was Lauren's decision. She didn't want him to think less of me. I tried to convince her otherwise, but she was adamant. I know I should have corrected the misconception, but I'm embarrassed to admit that I lacked the courage. Truthfully, I couldn't handle another son thinking poorly of me.

"What I never dared to consider was that maybe, just maybe, you were hurting too. I never fathomed that you might be able to forgive me for what I did. And I never dared to hope that you might still need me—at least not until this afternoon, when a fiery young woman was bold to knock on my door and demand to meet her future mother-in-law." Somehow, Adelle was laughing and crying at the same time. She looked over at her son and instantly sobered. "Braxton, I love you. I have missed you and your father dreadfully over the years, and I am so sorry for what I did and how I behaved. I can never get that time back. But I realized this afternoon that there was a slim possibility that I might still have a future with you—if you could ever find it in your heart to forgive me." Adelle searched his eyes, waiting for him to say something.

Finally, after what seemed like hours, Braxton looked up, and Adelle could see the tears in his eyes. "I've missed you too, Mom."

His mother rose slowly from the couch and enveloped her son in a warm embrace. Braxton stayed for two more hours, clearing up misconceptions and telling his mother a little about the gospel he believed in so fully. She was uncomfortable with the subject but listened and understood a little more about why her husband acted the way he had. They also filled each other in on the past decade of their lives, with Braxton finishing by talking about how he came to know Kennedy. Adelle was laughing heartily by the time he finished.

"She sounds wonderful, son," remarked his mother.

"She is." He nodded in agreement.

"You've forgiven her then?"

"How could I not?" Braxton chuckled, standing up. "But I'm still planning to let her stew about it for a few days. I need some retribution."

"Just don't let her stew too long, sweetheart." His mother laughed, following him to the door. "Let me just get my keys, and I can take you home."

Braxton smiled. "I'm pretty certain my truck is out front."

"Really?"

"Kennedy may be an interfering female, but she's a considerate one." He opened the door and gestured toward the street outside. "See?"

❊ Chapter 17 ❊

"So, Brax, when are you going to bring over this fiancée of yours?" Stefani asked as she placed a card on the table. "I'm the only one who hasn't met her."

"Soon." Braxton threw a card of his own down, waiting for Lauren and Jake to add their cards to the pile. "My hand," Braxton gloated as he swiped the four cards and added them to the pile he'd already accumulated.

"You're a hustler," Jake commented dryly as Braxton took the last trick, making it the third game in a row he'd won. "Either that or a cheater."

"Just because you can't play Rook, doesn't mean you should go around blaming others for your, umm . . ." Braxton's voice trailed off.

"Inadequacies," Stefani filled in. Braxton was her partner after all, so she was more than happy to agree. "He's right, you know. You really are playing like an incompetent fool, Jake."

"Hey, that's my partner you're talking about," Lauren defended.

"Great, I've been demoted from husband to partner," Jake grumbled, glancing at Stefani. "And don't worry about sparing my feelings, Stef. Just say it like you mean it."

"Who wants caramel corn?" Adelle walked in carrying a large bowl. She set it down on the middle of the table, and everyone quickly grabbed a handful.

"I'd forgotten how good your caramel corn tastes," Braxton said as he savored the treat.

174

"It's too bad Kennedy's not here to try it as well," Adelle stated pointedly.

"Maybe next time," Braxton murmured, grabbing another handful.

Lauren raised her eyebrows at her brother. "You know, you sure are being evasive whenever anyone mentions Kennedy's name. Why is that?"

Glancing at his watch, Braxton grabbed one final handful of caramel corn before pushing his chair back. "Well, it's getting late, and I've got an early meeting, so I'll see you all later."

"Braxton!" the three women yelled as he headed for the door. "'Night all," he called, and made a hasty escape.

It had been two weeks since Kennedy drove away and left him with his mother. At first, he was really upset with her manipulations. Why couldn't she just be patient and let him work things out with his family on his own? But then his conscience pricked, and deep down he knew that in all probability he would have remained a stubborn idiot forever. That's when he began to consider her viewpoint, and realized that she only interfered because she cared. After he came to that realization, he had no idea what to say to her. Every time he'd pick up the phone to call or get in the car to drive over to her apartment, his mind would go blank and he'd chicken out. What if she wouldn't forgive him? It's not like she'd made any moves to contact him. What if she'd decided that they weren't right for each other after all? What if she'd gone running back to Chris? He wasn't sure he could deal with that outcome, and so he simply did nothing but let his worry increase with each new day.

✳ ✤ ✳

Kennedy found herself fighting to stay awake at her desk. She could count the cumulative hours of sleep she'd had during the past two weeks on one hand, and she was exhausted. She still had not heard one word from Braxton and was becoming more depressed with each new day. Not knowing what else to do, she merely plugged along.

"Excuse me," a female's voice asked kindly. "Are you Kennedy Jackson?"

Jumping at the sound of her name, Kennedy stared guiltily up at the woman who had addressed her. She appeared to be in her mid-forties. She was tall and had short brown hair and an easy smile. Quickly placing her hand over the pad of paper she had been doodling on, Kennedy asked, "May I help you?"

"Yes, I was told to find you and let you know that I will be taking Shauna's place." She gave Kennedy a warm smile. "My name is Julia Sommers."

"Oh!" Kennedy practically jumped out of her chair. "It's so nice to meet you. I was told they had found a replacement, but no one ever told me when you were planning to start. I apologize for the lousy reception. I'm afraid I was daydreaming."

Julia laughed. "I'm happy to know I'm not the only one who doodles when I'm lost in thought."

Kennedy blushed, realizing she had been caught red-handed. "I'm so sorry. I'm between projects, and there hasn't been much for me to do around here the past few weeks. I've already color-coordinated all my paper-clips, and yours for that matter, as well as replaced all the real plants with silk. I hope you don't mind."

Julia laughed heartily. "Real plants are my nemesis. I think the longest I've kept one alive is two weeks, so you've done me a great favor. I think I'm going to enjoy working with you, Kennedy Jackson."

"Likewise," Kennedy responded with a grin as Julia stepped into her office, gesturing for Kennedy to join her.

As soon as they were both seated, Julia wasted no time with idle chitchat. "I've just been given a project that I'm going to need tons of help with if we are to get it finished in time. It is a gorgeous, multi-million dollar, 30,000 square-foot mansion in Scottsdale, and we, my dear, are going to decorate it to the hilt!" she exclaimed, flashing her brilliant white teeth. "Now, what do you say to that?"

Kennedy smiled radiantly, realizing why she had felt the need to stay at Interior Essentials. Here was the chance of a lifetime, and Julia seemed wonderful. Besides, she doubted Braxton could ever offer her this kind of an opportunity, not that he wanted her to work for him anymore. "You can definitely count me in."

"So, do you have any questions for me before we get started?"

"Actually, I do," Kennedy began hesitantly. "I don't mean to be nosy, but I've been dying to know what happened to Shauna. Do you have any idea?"

✳ ✺ ✳

"Mom, you're not going to believe this," Kennedy said when her mom answered the phone.

"Kennedy, is that you, honey?"

"Yeah, it's me. Don't you have caller ID?"

"Yes, but I'm not wearing my reading glasses. Believe what?"

"I found out what happened with Shauna," Kennedy whispered.

"Are you at work?" Olivia asked quietly.

"No. I'm in my car on my way home from work. Why?" Kennedy wondered.

"Why are we whispering?"

"I have no idea," Kennedy laughed.

"So, how did you find out? And what happened?"

"Oh, Mom, I got the most amazing new supervisor today. Her name is Julia, and she was very enlightening."

"Well, would you like to enlighten me then?"

Kennedy quickly complied. "In a nutshell, Shauna was initially hired based on a glowing recommendation that Mr. Caymen received from one of his colleagues. When the company began to receive some negative feedback from her clients, Mr. Caymen put her on a six-month probation. That was right before I started working for them. Evidently she failed and was let go."

"So, why was she so highly recommended then?"

"Turns out she was dating that particular colleague."

"The plot thickens."

"Yeah, in a way, I feel sorry for her now. Not only did she lose her job, but that guy broke up with her right before Christmas as well." Kennedy paused as she put two and two together. "Oh! That must have been what the flowers were for."

"What flowers?"

"Oh, uh, nevermind," Kennedy mumbled quickly before continuing. "Anyway, now she and the colleague are both out job hunting."

"So, how did Julia learn all of this?" Olivia asked.

Kennedy laughed delightedly. "It just so happens that come August, Julia Sommers will be Julia Sommers Caymen."

"Oh my!" Olivia exclaimed. "It's a regular soap opera at your office, isn't it?"

"Pretty much," Kennedy said. "I'm just so happy that I don't have to wonder anymore."

"Are you sure you want to continue working there?" Her mother sounded worried.

"Julia seems absolutely wonderful, Mom. She started her own design company years ago and met Mr. Caymen when he offered to buy her firm. Initially, she said no, but that led to one dinner meeting after another, which I'm sure turned into dinner dates at some point. When he finally proposed, they both agreed to a merger and *voilà*—I am now working as the assistant to a future partner."

"She chose an assistant with so little experience?"

"Thanks to Braxton," Kennedy said, her enthusiasm dropping dramatically with the reminder of him.

"Really?"

"Yes. Evidently he called Mr. Caymen to personally thank him for my work. He spun quite the story about my so-called amazing abilities and commended their company for having the foresight to hire me. He also included a generous bonus with his payment and suggested I get a new supervisor. One that could 'utilize my amazing talents.' At least that was Julia's version."

"Really?"

"Braxton was not one of Shauna's fans."

"Well, I know, but . . ." Her mother's voice trailed off as if she were lost in thought.

"I think he was planning on replacing Shauna anyway by that point, so after that, everything just fell into place."

"Did Braxton tell you what he did?"

"Of course not," Kennedy said. "You know he would never say anything. He's not one to point out his own generosity and kindness."

"I know, sweetie," Olivia replied. "What I was wondering is why he would think it's okay to interfere in your life without your knowledge—even though it did lead to a positive outcome," her mother prodded slowly.

Kennedy's eyes opened in wonder as her mother's words sunk in. "You're absolutely right, Mom! I never thought about it like that. Braxton is such a hypocrite!"

"Now darling, that's not what I meant, and you know it." Olivia remonstrated. "I just thought you might want to ask him about it," she said innocently.

"Believe me, I will."

✳ ❀ ✳

After saying good-bye to her mother, Kennedy deliberately missed the freeway exit that would take her back to her apartment and instead headed for the business offices of Taylor Homes, hoping Braxton would still be at work. She knew that his level of interference was not quite on par with hers, but she found this the perfect excuse to finally confront him, if for no other reason than to find closure. She'd found herself unable to concentrate or focus at work. Her mind flipped between worrying over a possibly broken engagement and daydreaming that Braxton would call or stop by, apologize for overreacting, and tell her he still loved her and couldn't live without her. However, with each passing day and no word from him, her worries had increased, and her dreams had diminished.

She didn't think she could spend one more day without knowing what he was thinking, how things had gone with his mother, and whether he wanted to terminate their engagement. The thought was downright nauseating. She loved Braxton. He was the right one for her. But he was part of the decision as well, and if he decided that she wasn't what he wanted, she would just have to accept that and move on. She did, after all, dig her own grave by being the meddlesome person she was. But she wasn't alone in that category, she reminded herself.

So, with trepidation, she drove directly to his office right after work. Seeing his truck in the parking lot caused her stomach to do flip-flops as she made her way inside to his office. Braxton's back was to her as he typed furiously on his computer. Pausing momentarily, he reached for a water bottle on his desk. As he was taking a long swig, Kennedy decided it was now or never.

"Hey." Her voice was quiet but firm, startling Braxton and causing him to choke and spill some water down the front of his shirt.

Once his coughing attack subsided, he glanced at Kennedy and then down at his wet shirt. "If only you could give me some kind of warning."

The comment brought a small smile to her lips. Immediately, though, she reminded herself that their relationship had changed, and she had no idea where she stood in his eyes. "Sorry to bother you. I just stopped by to bring you those floor plans I promised to take a look at." She sat a stack of papers on top of his desk. After standing there for several minutes, staring at the man she loved, she finally broke eye contact, glanced down at the floor, and waited for him to say something.

Instead, though, he got up, walked past her, and closed the door to give them some privacy. Kennedy watched him until at last their eyes met. Suddenly, she couldn't stop the words from pouring out of her mouth. "I'm so sorry, Brax. You were right. I had no business going to your mom's house and trying to make you mend fences you weren't ready to mend. I am a stupid, interfering person and I—"

Braxton had closed the distance between the two of them and put a stop to her speech by covering her mouth with his hand. "Shh," was all he said before he gathered her into his arms and his mouth came down hard over hers, passionately kissing away all the hurt she'd lived with during the past weeks.

When he finally pulled away, he looked into her eyes and said, "I love you, Kennedy Jackson. Please forgive me for being an idiot."

Kennedy hugged him back briefly before disengaging herself and slugging him in the chest. "Why didn't you call me then? For two weeks I have been in complete agony, thinking that any moment you were going to show up and demand the return of your ring."

He smiled as he pulled her to him. "You have to know that I could never live without you."

"You sure seemed to be doing a fine job of it these past two weeks!" Kennedy stepped back out of his embrace. Backing up to his desk, she hopped up to sit on it, crossed her arms, and glared at him. "And then I show up at work today to find out that Mr. Braxton Taylor, an active opponent of interference, actually meddled—yes, meddled—in my own business at work!" Kennedy was getting really worked up. "He won't forgive me for some necessary interventions, and yet he goes behind my back and calls the CEO of my company, bribing him with a bonus to get me a different supervisor."

Braxton waited for her to finish her diatribe. "Did it work?"

"Yes," she admitted grudgingly and then sarcastically asked, "Did things work out with your mom?"

"Yes." Fighting back a smile, he slowly walked toward her and took both of her hands in his. "Do you have any idea how much I've missed you, Kennedy Jackson?"

"No!" She tugged her hands free and said irritably, "I have absolutely no idea. You said you thought we got engaged prematurely and then slammed the door in my face. So, please, enlighten me."

Laughing, he relinquished her hands and walked toward the window, looking out in contemplation. "At first I was pretty angry that you would do something so underhanded, and I wasn't sure I could ever forgive you. But then I made peace with my mother and sisters, and by the time I realized and accepted the fact that you were right and I was wrong, I wasn't sure you'd want me back."

"I was what?" Kennedy melted, smiling broadly.

Shaking his head, Braxton chuckled and turned back toward her. "Please don't take this as the go-ahead to continue your interfering ways."

"My interfering ways?" She hopped off the desk and went to him, putting her arms loosely around his waist. "I thought I made it perfectly clear that we were both guilty of that particular offense," she teased.

"Yes, you did." Braxton grinned. "And I promise to never interfere again." He waited expectantly for her to make a similar promise.

"I'll try very hard to follow suit."

He chuckled. "I suppose I have to take what I can get. Besides, I've been busy catching up with my family. I owe you a rather enormous thank-you for bringing them back into my life." Braxton's hand gently caressed her cheek and tucked her hair behind her ear tenderly.

"I'm so glad to hear you've worked things out with them. I've been dying to know what happened with your mom."

"I figured," he said. "If you must know, we were able to clear up a lot of misconceptions, and things are good now—really good. They all keep badgering me about when I'll be bringing you over with me. So, are you free tonight?"

"I'll have to cancel my other date," she said.

"Brat." He leaned down to kiss her tenderly on the lips, drawing back only enough to murmur, "You know, it would be the cherry on top if you were to tell me you don't like your new supervisor and want to work for me instead."

"Umm, yeah . . ." Kennedy chewed on her lower lip, peeking up at him through her lashes. "About that . . ."

❋ Discussion Questions ❋

1. Kennedy is very reliant upon God for help throughout her life. She always tries to do the right thing, even if it doesn't make sense to her. Have you ever done something that didn't make sense because it felt right? How did it affect who you are today?

2. Braxton was quick to forgive the woman who killed his father, yet holds a long lasting grudge against his own family. Do you feel it is easier to forgive strangers than it is to forgive loved ones? How do you go about forgiving and learning to love someone who has hurt you?

3. Kennedy breaks her engagement because she feels it isn't right, even though Chris is a wonderful person and she is in love with him. Do you feel she is right to follow her feelings? What do you think about the idea that everyone has one perfect "soul mate"?

4. As Kennedy struggles with the decision to marry Braxton, her sister suggests she go for it, and if it is the wrong decision the Lord will let her know. How do you feel about this advice? Have you ever received an answer to prayer in this way?

5. Is there something Kennedy should do differently when Stacey is upset about Kennedy's relationship with Braxton? Would it be better for her to move out once she starts dating Braxton? Is she selfish to want a relationship with Braxton and a chance to keep her friendship with Stacey?

6. Does Kennedy go too far when she approaches Braxton's mother without his knowledge? Do you feel she is justified in trying to mend fences? What kind of situation warrants such interference, and what kind does not?

Photo by Kelly C. Christensen

Rachael Renee Anderson has always been an avid reader and a hopeless romantic—her favorite author is Jane Austen. In college, she started penning her own stories and discovered a love of writing as well. She graduated from Brigham Young University with a BS in business finance and a minor in psychology. She currently lives in Springville, Utah, with her wonderful husband, Jeff, and their four children. She loves staying home with her children and writing in her spare time. She also loves anything that can be done outdoors, including skiing, boating, biking, and gardening.

* ✳ *

Learn more about Rachael at **www.rachaelreneeanderson.com**, or email her at **rachael@rachaelreneeanderson.com**.